It's not unusual

*

Libby Fox

Copyright © 2018 Libby Fox "It's not unusual"

All rights reserved. No part of this publication may be reproduced, by any means, stored in a retrieval system, electronic, photocopying or any other form without the prior written permission of the author.

This is a work of fiction. Names, characters, events and certain locations are products of the author's imagination. Any resemblance to persons, accounts, events and places is completely coincidental.

About the author

*Libby Fox was born in Malta but lives in the Land of Robin Hood with her beloved husband David. She is mad about dogs, loves Classical Music especially Opera and enjoys singing (not necessarily in the bathroom). Currently she works as a Professional Interpreter. Three years ago she decided to put pen to paper. In between blushing and giggles she managed to write her first raunchy novel called "**BLACK FOR LAST.**" She persisted and wrote her second, may I say a still raunchier Sequel to her first called "**SOPHIE'S PARIS.**" Her third book "**CONFLICTS OF DESTINY**" is a different genre novel. Entertaining, funny, tearful at times but with an intriguing story set in Liverpool. It has been highly reviewed by Amazon readers.*

All her books are available in eKindle format as well.

To my very special husband David and just as special brother of mine Mario.

Don't judge a book by its cover.

Chapter 1
Chapter 2
Chapter 3
Chapter 4
Chapter 5
Chapter 6
Chapter 7
Chapter 8
Chapter 9
Chapter 10

Chapter 1

DORSET ENGLAND.

Julia Demarco was not an impulsive woman by any standards. Calmness and poise were virtues her friends and work colleagues had always recognised in her and genuinely admired. But that dull and weepy Saturday morning she could hardly contain her joy when her eyes fell on the pretty invitation to the twenty-first birthday party of her boss's daughter, Andrea. Seconds later she was on her phone to Lindsey.

"I'd not miss it for the whole world, Julia."

"I'm really excited about this one, you know."

"Just imagine the celebrities, dignitaries and kingpins from the Chamber of Commerce, everyone who is someone will be there for this exclusive occasion."

"And what about the venue, St. Just Castle. What a place to mingle with the prima donnas of the business world. It's exactly what the doctor ordered, don't you think?" Absolutely perfect, she thought.

The gilt-edged words echoed over and over in her heart. She inhaled musingly in satisfaction. So doing, her deep breath lifted her modest breasts enhancing their exquisite curves. Julia glared at them fleetingly as a plume of red hung over her cheeks.

"I see your little dream is still alive and kicking then."

Julia was secretly convinced this invitation could present her with the best opportunity yet to pursue her teenage dream if she played her cards right. Lindsey was right. They couldn't miss this for anything in the world and the summer break on the Spanish Costa could wait. Countless years she had toyed with the idea of owning her exclusive celebrity shoe Boutique, ideally somewhere in Paris or Milan. Or even New York or maybe London. But for now Devon or Dorset would be a good place to start.

"Well, this calls for new shoes and a new dress, Julia."

"I suppose so but I don't think I can afford another shopping extravaganza, I'm afraid. Don't forget Spain."

"Oh, Spain can wait. This is a once in a lifetime opportunity. Embrace it with both hands and why not get another small overdraft to help you out?"

But another overdraft was not an option this time. Of that Julia was adamant. If she was ever to cut it in the world of business she had to learn to keep tight grip over her finances. It wasn't rocket science. It just needed a bit of self-discipline and long-term planning and lots of common sense, of course.

So respecting the budget she set herself, Julia nonetheless purchased a modest pair of very elegant designer shoes and a red evening dress much the in colour for fashion at that moment. It had 'made to measure' written all over it, elegant, chic and perfect. Not only that, even the normally cavalier Lindsey showed some restraint and toned down her reckless streak. Needless to say, the stellar occasion at St. Just Castle was everything they had imagined and more, much more. Julia could not believe her eyes when they started to mingle with the array of distinguished guests, sipping her Champagne at delicate moments to lubricate her throat and smiling regally every time heads turned. The men's scrutiny tended to be more intense and lingered. Julia couldn't help blush a little.

One guest in particular, a tallish and not strikingly handsome man of a dark Mediterranean complexion, clad in black from head to toe, giving the impression of being a "*Mafioso,*" stalked her with his deep gaze as a tantalising smile danced on his full crimson lips. Unease chilled her heart like an unexpected cold shower. But with Lindsey by her side she felt she could maintain her self confidence. Lindsey herself was amused by the fashion parade on view, her eyes playfully springing from one female guest to the next verifying her painstakingly chosen dress was not replicated. But soon enough the enigmatic man in black too became an object of her scrutiny.

She immediately noticed no ring was in evidence on the significant finger of his left hand. But the shimmering vulgar medley of gold he wore around his neck, wrists and other fingers spoke volumes about the size of his assets. Equally formidable was the arrogant confidence his expansive forehead and unwavering blue gaze oozed.

Julia battled the literally dark off putting shadow damping her enthusiasm. She was starting to regret her presence at this upmarket event. Maybe she was being a little presumptuous mixing in with an elite company way above her status. But she didn't want to disappoint Lindsey. They had been best friends since she could remember and their friendship was as precious to her as her every breath. It was the best thing to ever happen to her.

"Have you noticed, Julia? You have an admirer. His eyes won't leave you alone. Are you going to acknowledge his close attention?"

"And then what Lindsey, what would I say to him?"

"You could smile for a start."

"But I don't even like him." fired Julia. "He's surely not my type."

Her emerald eyes had been a cocktail of sunshine and joy that morning. But for a moment her face turned into a pale sheet of steel beneath which lurked a feisty ego reinforced with grit and defiant determination. She knew she was standing on the threshold of an unfamiliar world dominated by ruthless arrogant men and she would need to dig deep and hard into her soul when she finally embarked on her little project. There would be endless pitfalls on the way. Unless she was prepared for any eventuality she would not last a single day.

She had vowed to rally every ounce of strength and every breath in her body to fight and defeat anything and anyone in her way. Nothing was going to stop her now from living her life-long dreams of seeing her baby come to life. If she was going to shake at the legs and melt away each time she was the object of a rich man's attention, then she had better forget it all and go back home.

"Hello."

It was the man in black who had lithely flitted across undetected and caught them unawares.

"Hello, ladies," he breezily announced, shaking their hands taking a long firm look around him before his intense gaze fell on Julia. His slick, striking bone structure enhanced the deep oceanic blue of his eyes beneath which seemed to lurk a fierce predator. His pursed lips softened the cold angularity of his face.

Julia desperately tried to avert her eyes but not without betraying her nervous disposition. So she withstood the onslaught resentfully. No doubt he was studying her carefully maybe pondering a devious strategy to make her his next seduction victim. For a fleeting second, his gaze rested on her lips, then devoured the rest of her body down to her red shoes, swiftly returning to her eyes.

"Hello," smiled Lindsey judiciously. "I'm Lindsey and this is my friend Julia."

Julia didn't know what to say or do but she resented not being allowed the time to introduce herself. Had she been allowed, she would have chosen a much colder tone from the start to distance herself and intimate to the man in no uncertain terms she was not interested in the least, no matter how vast his business empire was. He certainly was not her cup of tea and the longer he scrutinized her frame the more uncomfortable he made her feel.

"Franco Rocco, ladies, and I'm very pleased to meet you."

He loomed above them in his dark slick pinstriped suit straight from an exclusive Milan designer outlet. His broad shoulders and muscular arms eclipsed the distance between them. His azure gaze still lingering on her glossy lips then moved once more penetratingly into her stunning eyes. As if the sight of his immaculately white teeth wasn't intimidating enough he raised his hand and gently touched her arm to protect her from a clumsy waiter. Before she even had time to acknowledge his chivalrous gesture, her arm froze and her slender hand tightened into a firm grip.

She didn't know what hit her. Every nerve in her body stiffened sending a scorching current surging through her every vein followed by numbness. Momentarily she lost the power to move her limbs and it seemed his enormous hand caressed her arm for an eternity. This wasn't a good start at all. Her better judgement told her to brush his hand away, make up some inane excuse and take leave before she lost the plot completely.

"Hello," she said reluctantly. Her voice was hoarse and faint. She swallowed the air. Unable to regain her breath in time she rested her gaze on the luminous ring in his eyes. The electricity was mutual alright. He was obviously a seasoned charmer who got as much out of his act as he put into it. Yet his authority and poise never wavered. Unlike her, he was always in control.

"So, are you family, a friend of the family or ……"

She instantly recovered from her hesitant introduction. The blood inside her veins surged without a reason she could comprehend. It was evident he was a ladies' man but not her sort of man. She was convinced she didn't like him. She found brash men completely insufferable.

Nevertheless, by normal standards Franco Rocco was probably not an unattractive man. There was something distinctly charismatic about him. On reflection she could see why many women, maybe even Lindsey, would turn their heads and maybe even go weak in the legs. She wouldn't be surprised at all. But still, he was doubtlessly not her type and there wasn't a shadow of a doubt in her mind about her stand. Her first impressions had almost invariably been infallible.

Suddenly, an insatiable craving wreaked havoc inside her. She flushed a little when an army of butterflies fluttered inside her delicate stomach. It was a wild sensation she was unaccustomed to and was adamant she would have none of it. More so because Franco Rocco, a complete stranger, seemed to be the inexplicable cause of the wave of unfamiliar little stabs. She frowned, cupping her chin in the palm of her hand.

"I'm a close friend of the family and a former business partner. But now I'm the sole owner of a very successful chain of restaurants. As it happens I'm looking for someone outstanding to manage one of them."

"And you think you can find someone outstanding here, tonight?" Lindsey's voice betrayed an excitement not replicated in Julia's hardened eyes.

"I don't think Mr. Rocco is the type to mix business with pleasure, Lindsey." said Julia. Her lips stiffened. "Isn't that right Mr. Rocco?"

"Call me Franco please. Away with outdated formalities. I suppose it would be true normally."

Franco Rocco's was enjoying the sound of his intrepid voice, and his inflexible eyes.

"Success in business these days demands a huge amount of professionalism. You take your eyes off the ball at a strategic moment and you could damage your business permanently. But then again a high-flying entrepreneur cannot rule anything out. If the outstanding person I'm looking for is here tonight and I fail to notice him, then I'm the loser."

Julia butts in. "You said him. I take it you're looking for a male manager then?"

"On principle, yes of course. Experience has taught me that men normally take more quickly to my way of doing things. You've to lay out the structures leading to swift success and men comply more readily to preset procedures."

"A little bit sexist, don't you think?" frowned Lindsey.

"Sexist maybe from a female point of view but …" His broad shoulders broadened even more and his chest filled up. His uncompromising eyes smiled tauntingly.

"Sexist from all points of view, surely," Julia's horrified face shot an array of bullets at him. "Who says women won't make as good a job of managing your restaurant, if not better than men?"

The man in black may have had the financial clout but it didn't give him the absolute right to dismiss women as an inferior race, unable to manage his stupid restaurant. It was only a restaurant after all. It wasn't like running an international Space Station or a fleet of aircraft. Granted, she knew she was only a novice in the business world and knew precious little about how successful restaurants were run, yet she knew a fair amount about men and women. In the vast world of business men and women were still the same people who brushed shoulders on trains and buses, breathed the same air and shared the same earth. But petty prejudices were the product of narrow-mindedness and ignorance which had no place anywhere in the modern world, let alone in the business confraternity.

"I do." Franco's voice was firm. "I work with them every day. I'd know."

If he thought she was going to stand there acquiescingly listening to his arrogant prejudices against women, then he had something else coming. Like most men he had obviously been fooled by her gentle features and apparently soft-spoken way and had made rash assumptions about her docility.

"I take it you're not married then." Her unblinking eyes raged.

Franco's gaze stood still for a long moment in the shadow of his dark arched brows. It appeared she had succeeded in ushering him with a little surprise reaction. Being dwarfed by his towering frame instantly made her regret her impetuosity. This was an unexpected confrontation which brought back uncanny memories of a previous boyfriend while at University. He cajolingly bulldozed his way into her life, warts prejudices and all, and begrudgingly stumbled out of it soon after. But she had only been nineteen then.

"I'm not in fact. Was it my face or my pin-striped suit that gave it away?" he teased. His voice was calm and composed.

"Mr. Rocco you know full well some married men, when it suits them conveniently forget to wear their wedding ring."

"And obviously you don't think I'm one of them."

"Correct."

"So you must be a mentalist then."

"No, I'm not. I just won't be patronised by stuffy prejudices, that's all. I happen to think very highly of women because I work with them."

"You know, Julia, I believe we've both assumed a hostile stand here. I think we need a fresh start. Don't you think?" He looked fractionally at Lindsey who hadn't uttered a single word feeling terribly awkward and speechless standing between them.

She fleetingly exchanged a vacant look with Julia. Her lips pressed together in case a word slipped out which might cause even more damage. Then she contemplated on Franco's stern jaw in dismay, seriously thinking of starting to mingle on her own. Julia was obviously in a mood. "I don't think so," Julia stubbornly shook her head. Eager to catch his reaction her gaze impulsively fell on the jade iris of his irresistible eyes. She met a seasoned and implacable will behind his confident smile.

"I'm afraid you'll have to excuse us now, Lindsey and I need to find Andrea to wish her a happy birthday. I'm sure you'll want to mingle some more in search for your macho type manager."

"I won't disrupt your plans, ladies." Then with a look of amused conceit in his eyes deliberately steered towards Julia, "but I'm sure our paths will cross again soon. And I'm sure we can make a fresh start."

"You can always try, I suppose. But I wouldn't hold my breath if I were you."

"Is she always so belligerent?" He smiled at Lindsey evidently not expecting a reply. "Well it's been a pleasant challenge talking to you ladies. Something tells me you'll enjoy yourselves."

That night the two girls argued well into the small hours. Julia told Lindsey in no uncertain terms, Franco Rocco could have been the Donald Trump of Dorset for all she cared, she was not interested. She didn't like or fancy him; but above all disliked his misplaced arrogance. How dared he accuse her of belligerence? He'd only just met her for heaven's sake. If she ever needed to seek advice about her business plans he'd be the last person on earth she'd seek out. One thing Lindsey needed to understand was to let her do her own dating if she wanted to be part of her project.

"Julia, granted, he's a little arrogant, most handsome men are."

"Handsome! I don't think he's handsome at all."

"Okay, you don't think he's handsome. I beg to disagree. But he's a very successful businessman with clout and good advice who's taken the trouble to pick you out from the crowd. It's you he likes Julia."

"But I don't like him, Lindsey, and I've no intention of doing business with him. Can't you just leave it there and move on?"

"No, because I think you're missing out on an amazing opportunity. Wasn't that exactly why we went to Andrea's party in the first place?"

"No, the primary reason was Andrea's birthday. Anything else would have been secondary."

"He was right, you know. You two started on the wrong footing, that's all. Why not let him put things right?"

Julia's eyes instantly raged at Lindsey.

"Why do I feel you've done something I'll regret for the rest of my life? Lindsey what have you done?"

"Why not give him a chance, Julia? Let him show you his charming side."

"He hasn't got one, Lindsey. Full stop." she said unequivocally.

"Tell me you haven't agreed to something behind my back."

Lindsey smiled as she tilted her head towards her.

"Julia I've known you for a long time and you know I've grown to know you better than you know yourself. Sometimes, you don't seem to make any sense, you're too abrupt and intense. You instantly dismiss things before you've evaluated all the possibilities."

"Oh", Julia's arched brows froze for a second. "And you have?"

"Well what have you got to lose, tell me. This could be a very exciting moment in your life. You may be on the threshold of something big perhaps and fate has brought you together with a man who might make your future."

"What fate? He's an arrogant rich chauvinist who thought he might have his way with me. He knows girls normally drink themselves to oblivion at such parties and he thought he had the night sorted. That's all Lindsey. That's not fate. And I don't believe in fate anyway. What I believe in is hard work and the good sense to know a good thing when it presents itself. Believe me, this isn't it." Her eyes were as blunt as her words.

"Julia, before he left we exchanged mobile numbers. He's invited us out for a drink at his restaurant. That's all."

"Then you go." A touch of anger darkened her deep tones.

"Julia, it's not me but you he's interested in. You're the one with the business plan."

"My business ideas don't need any input from an obnoxious man who undoubtedly still thinks a woman's place is in the kitchen."

It took Lindsey a couple of weeks of persistent supplications before Julia, against her better judgement, finally surrendered and accepted to accompany Lindsey to Franco's restaurant. At the end she felt she was old enough to be sufficiently well-equipped to withstand men of Franco's ilk. Her sense of self-preservation was intact. Maybe a little show of civility might get him off her back and let her get on with her life's ambition.

One afternoon they drove up a winding hill flanked by a row of cute little houses with red roofs, overshadowed on the summit by a palatial residence with a lush drive leading to the entrance. The view of the harbour from that vantage point was breath-taking and Lindsey stopped the car to allow them the time to take it all in. The restaurant was at the bottom of the hill on the pier side. Needless to say it too enjoyed idyllic views to regale the often celebrity diners who regularly stopover, some of whom travelling long and far. The *Ristorante Bergamese* was in fact one of the most elegant eating places gracing the

Poole coast. It had built an unequalled reputation over the years for genuine Italian cuisine with particular sensitivity to regional delicacies. It was not unusual to meet patrons of Italian extract among its devoted patrons, some of whom hailing from towns as far as Rome and Milan.

"Hello ladies. Come in. Now that wasn't too hard, was it? I knew you would see sense eventually." Franco tilted his head, turned towards Julia, expecting a reaction. Quelling an odd pang inside her, she smiled politely hiding her displeasure. She tried to avoid his searching gaze which was starting to wreak havoc inside her. She was horrified at herself. Her customary wariness seemed to have gone dormant, given way to a host of unfamiliar impulses racing through her.

"Well, this is my favourite *ristorante* which I run with my older brother, Giuseppe. He's the one singing in the kitchen. I must warn you, he can be a little eccentric at times but he's a darling. And the ladies just adore him."

"I take it you haven't been here before?"

"Unfortunately, no I haven't," Lindsey gulped hesitantly. She had just realised the question was not addressed to herself but to her younger friend who had apparently monopolised their host's complete attention. She couldn't help notice Franco's warm smile gleaming across to Julia's eyes. She smiled too, willing Julia to warm to her somewhat unlikely admirer. " He threw his arms in the air and laughed politely.

"Well, it's always my great pleasure to welcome beautiful girls to our *ristorante*. I must add, you do look very beautiful tonight."

Julia felt a rush of blood shoot up her cheeks. Sweet compliments delivered in a deeply sexy foreign accent had always thrown her off her guard and she had never learnt how to deal with them. This should have been her cue to get the hell out of his haunt. This was not a good idea at all. She knew it. Indeed this fateful encounter could not only dent her ambition but reduce it to ashes.

The time their eyes met, Franco exuded a distinctive glow and sensed an irresistible mischief in hers.

"Charlotte. Will you come and serve our guests." His deep tones were uncompromising. Charlotte smiled respectfully and fulfilled her duties with impeccable charm and efficiency. As she took their order she smiled at them, a little condescendingly Julia thought, as if serving Franco's lady friends was a task she performed routinely. Evidently, she must have been very accustomed to the harem of girlfriends he doubtlessly lured to his haunt. A darker thought sent a sliver of humiliation through Julia's nerves and she was beginning to feel even more out of place. She looked across entreatingly but Lindsey was oblivious to everything apart from Franco's engaging profile.

Well, they were there now and there was no way out. Clearly this had been a huge mistake meeting him in his own back yard. If they had met in a neutral place then at least she would have had a chance to counteract his macho-laden beliefs and help adjourn them to modern day notions of equal opportunity. But with the only female on his payroll practically a teenager slaving behind the bar she didn't have a chance in hell. Firm restraint seemed the best option to adopt on the night.

"So, do you do this often then?" she asked crisply.

"How do you mean?" he retorted, calmly allowing the embroidered vowels to permeate the air.

"You know. Inviting girls like us for drinks and expecting us to be fascinated by your charm."

"Julia?" Lindsey blurted out. But she said nothing else having realised she had been brushed to the sidelines by the sparring protagonists.

"I'll take that as a compliment." His eyes glinted in a sea of blue as he surveyed her more rigorously, her clasped hands, her slick shoes, her pale lean legs and then her face, her lips and her fearful eyes. Franco's voice displayed tremendous vigour and self-confidence which doubtlessly played a key role in his career. One didn't run a successful establishment like "The *Bergamese*" by being timid and fearful of challenges. His eyes betrayed a streak of ruthlessness too.

"Well, if you meant do I pick up any odd girls from clubs as a hobby, the answer is in the negative. But do I invite interesting girls like you who I'd love to have as my cherished friends? Then, yes, of course. It is my business making friends when I like someone. Don't you think it's a noble pursuit?"

"If you say so." she said bluntly trying not to sound disappointed. How could he know she was interesting? She had deliberately rebuffed every word he had uttered.

He laughed. "So, won't you tell me something about yourself?"

What was there to say? There was nothing fabulously exciting happening in her life she would want to share with him, a mere stranger. She hadn't won any Olympic medals or climbed Mount Kilimanjaro or met anyone famous at any point in her life. She was just your average girl with an unexciting history. But with ambitions she really didn't want to divulge to him.

"What is there to tell? Nothing too exciting, I'm afraid." Her impersonal frown said it all. "One Sauvignon Blanc and soda, a diet coke, a small Cognac and mineral water," she said demurely.

"Thank you Charlotte."

"Pleasure, Mr. Rocco." She smiled, nodded gracefully and left.

"So, you were saying."

"Well, I'm an estate agent at the moment but not for long", she said reluctantly, with a deliberate nonchalance. "I've been there four years now."

"Here in Poole?" Franco sounded genuinely interested.

"No in Christchurch. I read for a degree in Tourism and Business Management but it's not really what I want to do."

"Oh," he said. "And where did you grow up?"

"I was born in the leafy part of Bournemouth." What she had hoped would come out sounding a little contemptuous ended up being cheeky and playful.

He laughed, nodded and said:

"Point taken Julia." Then, realising at that juncture he had completely overlooked Lindsey he turned to her.

"And what about you, Lindsey, are you from Bournemouth too?"

"Yes. We've been friends since primary school. Our families are very close too."

"Oh that's nice. So I take it you're from the leafy side of Bournemouth too."

The awkward tension which had hung heavy in the air seemed to have lifted and the words flowed more lithely with less antipathy.

"I'm afraid so. We're both posh."

"So," Julia broke out defiantly, unable to withstand the irksome conversation any further. "How many restaurants do you have?"

Franco grinned slightly bemused by her unexpected interest.

" I've three outlets, one in Edinburgh and my very first one in Bergamo. That's near Milan."

"So that's why you called this one *Bergamese.* Are you from *Bergamo* yourself?" Lindsey's delight lit up her eyes.

"Correct on both counts. You can imagine I've to commute regularly to keep an eye on all three. If one of them lets you down, all three tend to suffer and your reputation of course. That's why I need to choose my staff very wisely. In my absence they've to work as if I was there with them all the time."

"Is your menu different then from other Italian restaurants?"

"Your average patron would not normally notice anything different. But the short answer to your question is yes," As he replied he seemed to ponder Julia's face, his eyes wandering from neck to lips to eyes.

"You know some of the Milanese specialities were born in Bergamo. But Bergamo is only a little town if you like, so to say peripheral to Milan. The big towns always seem to monopolise the best ideas because that's where the money is."

"Why didn't you open a restaurant there then?" For a single moment Julia seemed genuinely drawn into the conversation. She was convinced there would be wisdom in his answer.

"The timing wasn't right, too much competition at the time." He paused to lubricate his lips. "You can't throw a new idea into the big world without a proper and extensive study of the market. And there's not much fun replicating something others have done." He paused once more and lubricated a bit more.

"But, enough about me. Now tell me Julia, you say you want to move away from being an estate agent. So are you looking at starting your own business then?"

Julia was shocked at the directness of his calculated conjecture? Could he really read her mind as quickly as that from the little she had given away? Was she already an open book to him? His reply scared her no end and she felt a strong compulsion not to answer. But she had to say something.

"I haven't really decided yet. I'm not in a hurry."

His smile was faint and bland though his intentions seemed crystal clear to Julia. He knew exactly he was spot on and was instantly preparing the groundwork for another social meeting. Wouldn't he just love to be her mentor?

As if he needed more proof of how clinical his shot in the dark had been, Lindsey's shocked face provided exactly that.

He leant over and whispered in Julia's ear:

"I find you very beautiful, you know. Not just pretty. There is something very desirable about you, a sort of sexual mystique." His soft purring, his closeness to her, his alluring aftershave, everything about him conspired to send hot flames across her cheeks. She couldn't even pull away from him fearing his powerful fragrance would pursue her to her bed. He seemed to be winning the battle of the senses.

"I love Chanel," he went on pursuing his strategy to ensnare her, his eyes resting on her peachy lips.

"Please stop." They were words bereft of any conviction.

"Your eyes are fascinating too."

Did the man have no shame? There were people around them. Lindsey, together with Charlotte and a restaurant packed with eavesdropping diners. She had to say something quickly to persuade him she was not this Barbie doll he was making her out to be. Or do something pretty quickly before her voice went completely numb. Charlotte's curious glances kept assaulting her integrity. She needed to stand up to him without seeming in any way brash or rude. Or maybe rude was the answer, get up and leave.

Franco picked up the mineral water and diluted his Cognac.

"Doesn't it spoil the brandy?"

"A little, I guess, I don't normally touch alcohol on duty. But today I made a little exception. After all I'm hosting two special ladies."

Julia suddenly rallied enough strength to stand up. She wasn't particularly tall but her lissom figure always stood her out not just to men's eyes. By any standards she was a remarkably beautiful woman. Any man would have thought so and Franco was no different. If anything, he was much more discerning then most when it came to stylish women.

"I think it's time to go now, Lindsey."

"Ah, but you must meet my brother before you leave. Let me call him.

You'll like him, you'll see."

Franco disappeared into the kitchen and came back almost instantly, raised eyebrows, the smile in his eyes tempered with irony.

"Sorry to disappoint you, ladies but it seems Giuseppe has popped out in search of something or other. Ah well, not to worry." His eyes sharpened.

"This means you must come back to meet him. You've to meet Giuseppe."

"Oh, it doesn't matter, Franco. At least we've met you properly now", she said impersonally.

"No, I insist ladies. You must come again. You must meet my brother."

"You've my number Franco." Lindsey didn't even dare look at Julia as she leant to kiss Franco on the cheek. She just hoped it wouldn't lead to a fall out.

"So are you impressed?" That stern smile reappeared on his lips, expectant, and it annoyed Julia immensely. Her eyes seemed unable to tear themselves away from the sway of his brutal mouth. It had become like a drug that stage-managed every movement of her eyes and it clearly wasn't a deliberate ploy on his part. More like an unconscious habit which did the damage nonetheless.

"So? I do expect a reply." A cold shiver ran down her spine at the severe tone of his voice. "Yes." she nodded. "We're impressed." She looked at Lindsey smiling politely but Lindsey having been marginal to the main event all night simply nodded.

"Oh, the royal we, but I was asking you. Are you impressed Julia?"

"I know very little about you." She let out somewhat wildly and indignantly. She barely had time to regret her sudden loss of control before he expertly raised his stake.

"Good. Then how about dinner here next Friday just you and me? I can't think of a better way to get acquainted properly."

"Thank you very much but I don't think so. She pulled herself together desperately avoiding his hypnotic blue gaze.

"What have you got to lose, Julia? Think about it. Promise me you'll make your mind up." She wished she could ignore the growing queasiness inside her and say yes just to get him off her back. But she knew it would have been a fatal mistake. He was not the type to give up and forget about her. It had been a gross misjudgement on her part to have gone there with Lindsey in the first place because now she had raised his hopes. Now he would not leave her alone.

"So, you'll think about it then?"

"You don't have to, really. Bye and thanks," She said, as she left the restaurant without even checking if Lindsey was following behind.

For a reckless number of hours Franco's chiselled features clung to the walls of Julia's mind like a barnacle. She lay in bed desolately staring at the dark featureless ceiling and it scared her to be spending a sleepless night thinking of a man she didn't even like. It was well into the small hours when she eventually fell asleep; her heavy blond head nestled restfully on pillows of soft goose down.

The following day at the office, she sat in front of her monitor, sipping a cup of tea and running through a list of clients to set up her next appointments for the week. Then suddenly a voice tore through the deep calm.

"Hello. Good morning Julia?"

It was Franco. The shock coupled with his silky tones had a mesmerizing effect on her. Unlike the previous occasions he looked awesomely handsome and his seductive expensive aftershave sent a florid fragrance across the room. It was a potent scent of red roses, freshly cut just for her. Everything about him was serene and surreally classic. His bronzed angular face, jet black mane simply brushed back with a hint of gel, silk black shirt and matching tie, shimmering smart shoes and a cute behind.

There was much more than sexual aura though that stood Franco apart from other men. His undoubted successful ventures can't have been due solely to his business acumen. His character, ruthless and formidable but equally scrupulous and steadfast, she had to admit, had a lot to commend it. Above all his blue eyes oozed a sea of power and influence normally the endowment of army generals.

Julia could hardly sit still. Her legs were shaking, her heart pounding and her gaze fastened to her clasped hands. She struggled to dispel her frenzied thoughts. This was a dangerous game torturing her mind, knowing her bashful frame visibly pleasured his wistful gaze.

Although she bordered on being small there were times when she looked and felt like a towering goddess. Sadly this wasn't one of those moments.

Chapter 2

"Surely, you're not here to book a viewing?"

"No, no, no, Julia. I have no intention of adding to my portfolio."

"Then, what do I owe this surprise visit to?"

"I was in the vicinity so I thought I'd pop in and say hello. I hope that's okay with you."

Julia sent him a startled look. There was no point asking him how he found her office. It was obvious albeit regretful. She wondered what other little surprises he might be harbouring behind that prominent forehead of his. Surely he hadn't come to insult her by offering her a post as barmaid in his exclusive restaurant. Or had he perhaps redefined his beliefs and notions about the place of women in his establishments and come to make her his manager?

She had disliked his arrogant and bigoted manner the moment he set his eyes on her. But as he stood in front of her at that moment, looking so affably fresh and fragrant, full of civility and charm, she was finding it very hard to sustain her *bête-noir* image of him. For a long moment she could not avert her eyes from the hardened bow of his mouth, tempered as it was by the soave blue of his crystal eyes.

She quickly decided his impromptu visit was a desperate attempt on his part to orchestrate a sort of sequel to his next social encounter. Not if she could help it though and she still had no intention of changing her mind despite Lindsey's apparent defection. Trying to avoid his constant gaze she nervously kept drawing a deep breath. Then she felt the silent presence of her colleague across the room whose transfixed gaze flitted from him to her and back to him like a spectator at Wimbledon. A cocktail of emotions, embarrassment, anger, disappointment and frustration mingled in her heart. But against all odds one thing was certain, she had to stay firm, calm and confident.

A tiny shiver betrayed a temporary frailty in her as a sea of fire rose to her cheeks. She instantly braced herself, outwardly and inwardly. She was thankful Lindsey had taken the day off with a stomach complaint.

"I'll tell you why I'm here. My brother was very disappointed to have missed you the other night. You must know he is a bit of a ladies' man and a very popular one too, may I add. He is the sweetest and most gregarious creature on this planet. He wants to meet you so he suggested I should invite you over again for drinks and dinner this time. He promised he would make you the best ever *'penne rigate alla puttanesca."* Now that was a dish she had never had or even heard of. She looked at him incredulously. This was certainly not what she was expecting to hear, another charming invitation on behalf of his brother. But a voice inside her told her she shouldn't take his offer on its face value. Why would his brother be interested in her at all? As far as she knew he was happily married and seemingly in his sixties. There had to be an ulterior motive. It made sense. The whole situation seemed so amateurish and manufactured. Yet, although she was hugely suspicious of the whole thing, somewhere in her head, in a little remote corner, was starting to intrigue her in an odd sort of way and this was what scared her more than Lindsey's indiscretions or Franco himself.

"And how old is your brother?" She asked pointing her chin at him.

He laughed in a most natural manner, softening the curves of his sexy mouth and sending an instant twinge into the pit of her stomach. Almost unconsciously she glanced at his face and heat intensified all over hers.

"Well, I wouldn't worry about that. He's certainly very married. He just loves to entertain, worships the company of women, any old excuse will do and he is the genuine thing."

Just like you then, Julia wanted to add rather bashfully. But to her relief, her better judgement prevailed.

"You see, it brings him out of the kitchen. Though he is an accomplished chef, he probably loves cooking more than he loves his wife and me put together, strange as it may sound he gets a little claustrophobic sometimes in the kitchen. His real joy is meeting people and sharing his stories and his new culinary creations. He loves to play to an appreciative audience. You'll see, Julia. He's a gem. You'll love him."

Resentful of the way she kept undermining her opposition she nonetheless couldn't see how she could decline his invitation put to her in such seductive manner. But suspicions of a hidden agenda lingered. She knew she couldn't trust him despite the clear ocean flowing from his eyes.

She hesitated for a long second, glancing around, biding her time and weighing what she was about to say. "So," it was a remorseless tone which truncated her pause. "If you think you can manipulate your way into my bed, I think you'll be very mistaken," she blazed at him, "even if you enlist your brother's help."

"Honestly, Julia." It was a masterly stroke. A touch of contempt invaded his smile.

"Do you really think I'm so shallow? You've a body to die for, I know, no man would argue with that I can assure you. If I was after a one night stand surely by now it would all be done and dusted with, don't you think?"

"No. I don't Franco. People who know me know I'm not the type to entertain one night stands. If you had bothered to ask Charlotte, your devoted barmaid for her opinion she would have told you."

"*Touché*, but what I'm really interested in is not your bed but your heart." He laughed again and shook his head gracefully. Then he deliberately rested his eyes on her lingeringly, giving her goose bumps. Her skin tightened while she felt inside her the churn of a volcanic cauldron burning mercilessly.

"So you're telling me you've never done this sort of thing before and you want me to believe you? A man in your privileged position who must meet pretty girls every night at your restaurant? I know you may seem very handsome to some girls."

"Julia, I didn't come here to argue or to manipulate you. I don't do mind games, or one night stands. But enough said for now. So, we'll expect you Friday night. Believe me you'll make my brother's day and mine of course. I think you and I can be friends."

He smiled, wished her colleague a good day and left in an elegant swagger. As he left, she felt instantly relaxed, almost subconsciously. Their short-lived acquaintance had suddenly turned into a battle not so daunting after all. If playing with him at his own game was what was needed to get him off her back, then so be it. What did she have to lose? So he hadn't come to insult her with a cheap job offer after all.

Driving home that evening, she was much less relaxed. A host of familiar and unfamiliar thoughts tormented her so much. At one moment she almost lost control of her vehicle. She felt to be dreaming with her eyes wide open. The car swerved vehemently to the left. The tyres screeched and treaded on to the pavement, she slammed her foot on the brakes and juddered to a standstill kissing the curb.

Shaking all over she dropped her eyelids and clenched her fists in frustration. Then she gasped deeply, reeling from the ragged pain in her back. She sat dazed, motionless and silent, thinking about nothing. She had never believed nothingness could occupy her thoughts so ruthlessly. An odd feeling was wrenching her soul apart. A sharp pain in her neck brought her back to earth. She pulled a grimace. Her cautious green eyes veered to the right and left. Not a soul in sight at least she thought. Her fingers clinched the steering wheel again. She precariously sat back ignoring the appalling pain clamping the root of her spine. The sinews in her neck creaked. What's wrong with you she asked herself, frowning at the rear-view mirror?

On top of all that the pain in her soul stayed on for long hours through the night. Her confidence as a driver too had taken a terrible knock. She had never before allowed herself to be so shaken while driving. She could have hit someone or even seriously injure them. Why had she allowed her thoughts to distract her so irresponsibly? So Franco had invited her over again. She was convinced he had something up his sleeve, maybe a job offer she couldn't refuse. But she was equally adamant she would refuse it without even considering it. There was no harm in that. So why did she feel so annoyed, so frustrated? He had requested to be her friend. She'd rather have him as her friend than her adversary. As a friend she was confident she could handle him and his brother too. She would never have to face his dark side if indeed he had one.

Deep down she knew she had the mettle to enable her to withstand a sort of arm-wrestling bout in pursuit of her business dream. She painstakingly rehearsed as if for a job interview, gruelling herself and planning apt responses to outdo Franco's strategies. Apart from being an accomplished businessman, she now knew his innate charm and power of persuasion. She was going to need every inch of her steely grit to keep his devious sway at a safe distance.

Before retiring to bed she had one indelible question hanging in the corridors of her mind. Should she call Lindsey to ask her to go with her? She was her bosom friend after all. She was in two minds yet she knew perfectly well she would be a stronger person on her own. Lindsey would only get in the way. Maybe this time she would do it alone. It was about time she stood up to be counted without relying on outside help.

Although she found it hard to banish the ring of Franco's laugh from the forefront of her thoughts, she strangely harboured excitement at the prospect of another challenging encounter.

Naively she tried to convince herself it was the prospect of meeting Franco's brother that thrilled her. But as she sat down to read her magazine, Franco's blue eyes and mysterious smile clung to every page like a huge billboard portraying his tanned face. She desperately prayed his terrifying charm would not permeate her dreams too.

Then Lindsey rang eager to exchange a bit of gossip. She was feeling much better. It was a welcome distraction for Julia.

"Lindsey, guess who turned up at the office today?"

"Man or woman?"

"Man of course."

As friends of long-standing both had been there for each other through thick and thin, in good times and bad. They even had sworn to be friends for ever. But lately Julia was finding their friendship hard work and ever so trying at times. It was beginning to feel like a marriage void of soul and dynamism.

"Franco, he has asked me to meet his brother."

"And …?"

"What do you mean and?"

"You want me to come with you?"

Julia's suspicions were growing that Lindsey herself might in fact have orchestrated Franco's unexpected visit. But there was little point making accusations she couldn't prove and relegate their prized friendship to a cold spell. Her unsubstantiated suspicions however helped restore her cool-headedness. It brought her priorities back into perspective and dispelled those annoying imaginary billboards. It also restored her confidence in herself.

"So when is the invite for?"

"This Friday," her voice was matter-of-fact, no frills.

"Oh, I can't wait, Julia. What shall I wear? And what are you going to wear? I think I'll get another pair of shoes."

The line seemed to go dead for a second or two.

"Julia? Are you still there?"

"Lindsey."

"I thought the line had gone dead on us."

"Lindsey, I'll be honest with you. I wasn't going to tell you anything about this, you know, because I need to do this on my own."

"How do you mean, on your own? Why?" Her hearty tones were stunned by shock and disappointment.

"Are you starting to like him then? Has his charm got to you too?"

"Lindsey, don't be silly. Maybe there's a side to him which I don't find unpleasant but he's much too arrogant and self-opinionated to impress me."

Julia wondered why she was even responding to Lindsey's absurd assumptions. Franco simply wasn't her type. She thought it was pretty obvious from the first minute they met. Surely, Lindsey knew and should have acknowledged it.

"So why would you still want to go on your own Julia?"

"The thing is, my darling, he's not interested in you unfortunately. I would love it to bits if he was but you know very well it's not going to happen. I want to go on my own because I want to sort this out once and for all before it derails my dream plan. There is no room for him in my life at this time and he must understand it and leave me alone."

The implication could not be more obvious. Lindsey would end up being his ally once more. She took the hint. What she did not expect though was the following dig.

"Lindsey if you're really after a one night stand with Franco you'd not want me around, would you."

"Julia, are you serious?" Lindsey did not sound in any way distressed by the cheap jibe, more surprised than shocked.

Julia regretted it immediately but maybe it had to be said.

"Well, you did admit to fancying him."

"I guess I asked for that. Well, I hope you know what you're doing. Do call though if it fails and you happen to need my assistance."

"You'd think a man of his intelligence and discerning would know I'm not interested", she firmly said.

"So, why are you even going then?" Lindsey's persistence was starting to annoy her, making her feel even more uneasy about the whole thing.

"Because Lindsey, you for one should understand that I can't just run away as if I was afraid of him. And it's about time a woman stood up to his insufferable sexist prejudices."

"And you think you can make him change his attitude in one evening?"

"No. But I'll certainly show him how wrong and antiquated his views are."

"Well I can only commend you for that", Lindsey's quiet tones lacked conviction. "And I do wish you luck, Julia."

"Lindsey, you can't win anything in life by running away from a problem. And at the moment he's a problem. He'll pursue me and haunt me until he gets his way if I don't nip it in the bud and put this thing to rest now." She regretted her awkward choice of words. "That's what men do as if you didn't know. More so if he thinks I'm afraid of him. I'm not afraid of him. I do hope you don't take this personal, Lindsey."

"No fear of that Julia. What are friends for after all? But if you change your mind, you know where to find me."

"Okay, Lindsey. Don't worry, I'll be fine."

On Friday evening as the sun sunk into the ocean Julia drove down to Poole and parked the car just outside Franco's restaurant. She allowed herself a self-indulgent smile. Took a deep breath to brace herself for what she hoped would be a learning experience which would serve her well in her future dealings with businessmen. But as soon as she stepped inside all the steely confidence she had rallied for a battlefield mindset abandoned her. She dithered at the entrance staring at diners when it suddenly hit her, even more brutally than before, Franco and his brother were mere strangers to her. Despite her dogged determination to fight her corner, however admirable her cause seemed to her, she was nonetheless dealing with a ruthless and proven master. She was a mere pawn in his experienced hands.

There she was standing all alone on unfamiliar territory armed with nothing more than a crusading ego, an ephemeral childhood fantasy and her ridiculously pretentious red dress. She took a deep breath and told herself to stand tall and firm. Then she focused her mental resources into summoning that smidgen of showmanship worthy of her loud dress. She smiled regally at an elderly couple who stepped in ahead of her, braced herself once more and followed them. She calmly stepped up to the bar, sat on a high stool beside the couple then ordered a Campari and soda. She looked over her shoulder around the restaurant. It was still relatively quiet. There was no sign of Franco or his brother anywhere. A couple of smart, indolent waiters surveyed the sparsely sat diners indulging in the early-bird meal deals.

As she sipped her Campari, in a desperate bid to kick-start her flagging confidence, she kept reminding herself how impervious to pressure she had been in the past. Hang on in there Julia; she whispered to herself as her taut limbs loosened. A feeling of well-being started to permeate her veins, her heart and her thoughts.

"Hello," The middle-aged woman smiled.

"Oh, hello. Good evening. How unsociable of me. I was miles away," Julia apologised.

"Hello," said the gentleman standing next to his wife.

"I'm John and this is my wife Jean."

"I'm Julia pleased to meet you."

" Are you waiting for your date then?"

"No, no, nothing so romantic I'm afraid", Julia was quick to point out. "I'm on a sort of business mission I suppose. I'm meeting Franco's and his brother."

"You're not buying the restaurant, are you? We can tell you, it's very popular and successful. We've been coming here since it's opening, oh, how many years ago would that be now dear?" His elongated grey eyes below his matching arched eyebrows stood still in anticipation.

"Oh, I can't remember, John, ten maybe." Her initial embarrassment metamorphosed into a jolly smile.

"We were also good patrons at the old venue, you know, on Queen's street. Mind you, early evenings on certain weekdays can be relatively quiet. Some people are more continental in their habits these days you know. But as the night wears on it always gets busier. However, the food here is the main event as no doubt you'll find out. It is always extraordinary good, so is the service." He smiled at his wife as if to underline their joint satisfaction and then returned to Julia.

"John, she's too young to get mixed up in this restaurant madness."

Suspecting Julia might be feeling a little intimidated, his wife punctuated the brief silence with an apologetic smile.

"Excuse my husband, Julia." But before Julia nodded she went on. "Sometimes I really don't know where he gets these random assumptions from. His logic never ceases to baffle me." Then she frowned comically at him. "And he hasn't as far as I know touched any alcohol yet." she added, momentarily arching her pencilled eyebrows even more. Then she planted a loving kiss on his lips and a sense of sheer delight returned to her eyes. Her husband discharged a cocktail of puzzlement and joy and said nothing. He just raised his beer glass lovingly and took a long sip. It was evident there was mutual understanding in their seemingly quirky relationship. It was a loving and light-hearted one, judging by her first impression, a very happy one too.

"It's alright. I'm hoping to open a designer shoe store one day. But at the moment it's just an idea in its infancy."

"So you must be very excited. Don't tell me, you've come here tonight to pick Franco's brain. Tell me I'm right."

"I'm afraid you're wrong."

"Stop harassing the lady, John." The exasperation on her face spoke louder than her words. "You're very beautiful, you know." She smiled suitably at Julia as she gracefully adjusted a stubborn curl.

"I fully concur with my wife's expert judgement," John nodded and raised his glass to Julia. "Cheers."

"Cheers." Julia felt much more relaxed now. "And thanks." Julia felt much more relaxed now. Talking to the old couple had a soothing effect on her nerves. Also it had been infinitely better than sitting on her own waiting. Waiting in silence would have allowed her most fearful thoughts to weaken her resolve and summon every possible reason why she shouldn't be there. The barman didn't seem the type to make intelligent conversation either. This was the perfect tonic to help her sharpen her wit and her sword. She was convinced Franco was prowling somewhere in the kitchen. Probably inspecting her every move and listening to every word she said as he put the final touches to his strategy for the night.

"Now if I'd been 20 years younger ….."

"Stop it John. You're embarrassing the young lady, and me."

Jean's intervention was as firm as it was immediate.

"Oh it's okay, honestly. I'm fine." Julia shook her head, topped her Campari with more soda and took a lazy sip. "I really admire a couple like you, if you don't mind me saying so. You obviously love each other very much and know the secret of a lasting marriage."

"Very simple," John was quick to respond. "The answer is a candle-lit dinner at a choice restaurant twice a week, I go on Tuesdays, the wife on Thursdays. *Voilà*. Unfortunately, it's her birthday today."

Julia laughed at his daring and ready humour. She found him endearing if quirky. If he'd been 20 years younger and single, maybe she would have been seriously tempted to date him.

"You see what I've to put up with? But he's the love of my life and that's exactly why I'm still married to him."

"You're a very lucky couple, you know."

"Tell her, tell her." John chuckled.

"I'm really pleased to have met you tonight. I'm sure younger couples have a lot to learn from you."

"So, is there a man in your life then?" asked Jean as delicately as she could. Probably to forestall her husband, fearing he would have done it much less tactfully. The look in his eyes confirmed her suspicions.

"Not at the moment," Julia smiled awkwardly.

"Don't wait too long then," John tapped his finger in the air to make his point. "Or the good ones will all have been taken. It's not good to settle for second best."

"John," snapped Jean. "Behave yourself."

Julia suddenly didn't like where the conversation was going and wished Franco would show up soon. Maybe she should announce herself to the barman before her confidence flagged once again. But she didn't have to. Franco's looming frame appeared at the entrance at that very moment and slowly approached her.

A sly anticipation tickled her nerves increasing in intensity as he got closer. Her eyelids dropped and she reluctantly surveyed her sleek red cotton dress, tight around the hips and hardly an inch below her knees. How she could have spent forty minutes to make such an unwise choice of dress, she would never understand. It had been so uncharacteristic of her. She had practically never taken so long before or been such an indecisive wreck.

The last time it had happened was when she'd gone out on her first date. Even then she had made the wrong choice of colour and the date hadn't gone too well either. It would have been so much better to have opted for subtle elegance instead of exuberance. A fluid white blouse over her flowing beige cotton dress she had bought in Barcelona would have been fine and much less pretentious. It seemed so simple now.

Something in her stomach fluttered. She shrugged her shoulders and felt a thin film of sweat over her forehead as the predator's eyes met hers. A sharp-edged sensation tore through her, awakening animal instincts she had forgotten still inhabited her body. Her excitement grew. But she was scared. Why, suddenly, was all this havoc running riot inside her. Franco hadn't made the slightest impression on her the first time he had approached her. She had found him quite annoying, shallow and pompous. So why was his presence having such a devastating impact on her now? The skin on her temples was weeping tension. She grasped her glass in desperation and swallowed so quickly that she almost choked. She coughed erratically.

"Are you alright? Would you like some water?"

Not the introduction she had rehearsed in her mind. As Franco and the elderly couple watched an odd inner compulsion came to her assistance. She managed to keep her wits and her composure and sat motionless for a long moment like vulnerable booty waiting for the merciless predator to pounce.

"I'll be fine, thank you."

"Have you been waiting long?"

"Only a few minutes, I've been in very pleasant company with John and Jean here."

"Ah, good. But has Giuseppe not come out to welcome you?"

Franco hardly gave Julia time to respond. He instantly waved his finger in the air and with a firm nod dispatched the immaculately groomed young barman into the kitchen with military deference. Any casual visitor to the Bergamese couldn't have missed Franco's aura of power and respect and the incomparable discipline with which his employees responded. Small wonder he was such a successful and esteemed entrepreneur.

It was only a matter of seconds before Giuseppe emerged and rushed to meet Julia with a profusion of apologies accompanied with a "*joie de vivre*" she had rarely witnessed.

"*Buona Sera Signorina.* So finally I get to meet the beautiful princess. Now I understand why my brother can't stop talking about you," he went on, a warm smile of approval breaking out.

"I'm really thrilled to meet you, Miss Julia." He shook her hand with an unmistakably genuine passion in his watery eyes.

"Thank you. You're very kind."

"I've prepared something very special for you tonight, *Signorina* Julia. Please follow me into the kitchen and I'll show you."

"Giuseppe, Giuseppe easy, easy. Our guest has only just arrived. She's not a student at your cookery class, you know."

Franco's reassuring eyes covered Julia with a stark and primeval possessiveness, setting off a sharp jolt of excitement inside her.

"Of course, I'm sorry, *Signorina*. But I've a little surprise for you in the fridge."

Surprise, she thought. She didn't know whether she really wanted any more surprises. In fact, at that moment the entire purpose of her visit evaded her. What exactly was she doing there on her own? Why had meeting Franco's brother suddenly become a major event? The whole thing had been a terrible mistake. It wasn't as if Giuseppe was a fashion guru with an expertise in designer shoes. He was just a chef for heaven's sake, an accomplished one at that evidently but nonetheless a chef, not quite the area of expertise her immediate remit prescribed.

"You see, Miss Julia, I've just come up with my own take on a traditional '*Cassatella*'. It's an Italian sort of torte, very popular in Sicily and southern Italy. And I'm hoping you've a sweet tooth."

Suddenly, from a scared incognito at the bar she was catapulted to the rank of chef's special guest, and awarded the privileged brief of connoisseur taster for his new patisserie creation.

Well, you make me feel very special. Thank you, I'm flattered. I must admit I'm partial to chocolate gateaux especially with a generous helping of double cream. But my waistline doesn't approve any more."

"*Signorina*, once a week you're allowed to spoil yourself rotten. I assure you I don't use a lot of sugar in my cooking."

A waiter approached and courteously invited John and Jean to their table.

"It's been nice to meet you Julia and we hope to meet you again soon."

"Yes, I'll look forward to that", Julia smiled and politely nodded to the departing couple.

"Enjoy your evening", said Jean as they were led away.

Franco waved one of his attendant waiters over and ordered a bottle of seasoned vintage, a ritual the young man was obviously well-rehearsed in. He then led Julia and Giuseppe to a secluded table overhung by a beautiful fresco of the Sorrento coastline. They sat down and imbibed an exceptional bottle of aged Barolo over a selection of garlic *ciabatta* and olive *focaccia* as the conversation flowed effortlessly.

What had started as an uncomfortable encounter for Julia was blossoming into a thoroughly fascinating and complete evening, highlighted by a string of charming and funny anecdotes, a delicious *pâtisserie* and a superb bottle of wine picked by a seasoned connoisseur. The Giuseppe factor, no doubt, had worked a treat and had pulled the whole thing off for Franco. What a consummate ploy it had been.

She couldn't believe how all her fears, worries and reservations had unwittingly cowered. Magically replaced by a colourful mosaic of idyllic memories of a nostalgic Italy where scooters, teenagers and pizza parlours reigned supreme. Spurred on by the tenderness of the occasion and the invigorating nature of the wine she felt helplessly compelled to open up.

"Can I pick your brain about something?"

She must have caught Franco off guard because she couldn't help notice how the enlarged pupils of his eyes suddenly stood still. As he made no visible attempt to reply to her request she went on.

"I'm hoping to open a ladies designer outlet for shoes, I don't know where yet, it's only an idea at the moment." Her voice was withdrawn but firm.

"I say this is a surprise." The smile in his eyes was genuine and warm. "So you think you've what it takes to be a business woman."

Her voice failing her for a moment she simply nodded. She was incredulous at the ease and fluidity of their exchanges and how well they had got on all evening. But she couldn't allow her relaxed attitude to overwhelm her cool-headedness.

"So, what exactly do you want to know Julia?"

This was too perfect to be true. He hadn't made one single pass at her all night. Granted his brother's presence might have had something to do with it. She had to hand it to him; he had conducted himself with the supreme tact of a true gentleman, by any standards. But despite everything she suspected that a powerful and accomplished businessman of the likes of Franco was not going to let her off so lightly. Ruthlessness was an integral part of a successful entrepreneur, be it in business, politics, love or whatever. At that moment Franco's mobile rang.

"You'll have to excuse me, Julia. I shouldn't be too long." He smiled at her and walked away. Giuseppe waited till he had disappeared into the kitchen before he offered Julia a Cognac.

"I guess in these times of political correctness, only Cognac from France has the right to that name. What I'm about to offer you though, is a Brandy made in Italy, a Stock 84 said in Italian as '*Ottanta Quattro*'. He stepped behind the bar and swiftly returned brandishing a golden bottle bearing the said label. He graciously poured the syrupy liquid into a largish Brandy glass and in his younger brother's brief absence he candidly opened up.

"You know, Franco is just like our father used to be. He reminds me of him all the time. He feels it's his sole responsibility to see to everyone's needs in the family and in the business. He has a heart the size of the queen's bank account. And he can be a very daunting figure when it comes to keeping order and running the restaurant. He's firm and sometimes critical when he needs to but fair. He's always fair. That's why he's so successful and everyone likes him."

Julia sipped the Brandy. It had quite a distinctive taste albeit coarser than her regular alcoholic favourites. But then she was not a seasoned Brandy drinker. Though it was a taste she could easily get used to and was seriously tempted to stock it in her own drink cabinet. She almost made a pun about wanting to stock a 'Stock 84' but she refrained.

"As you know all bosses need to be firm to command respect. But he always knows the right dose and he's never abusive or unkind. Everyone feels he really cares and he has a soft spot for …."
"I noticed he smiles a lot too." Julia swiftly said not sure whether she really wanted to know what Franco's soft spot was. Giuseppe was a real darling. He obviously thought very highly of his younger brother and it seemed probably of her too. But she could surmise what he was trying to do. She suspected it had all been choreographed by Franco himself to create the perfect stage. Perhaps he thought being marooned on his

territory would make her more vulnerable, weaker and overawed. Vulnerable maybe, but weak no, not anymore.

Even though she was truly falling under Giuseppe's spell, she wasn't going to allow herself to be honey-spooned and groomed like a lamb for the slaughter. Indeed she loved Giuseppe's Latin warmth and his charming anecdotes that created a natural ring of intimacy around them. She could gladly listen to forever. She was genuinely flattered by the way the evening had blossomed and nothing could have been farther from the date she had braced herself for.

But despite all the pleasantries and all the fuss they had made about her, she was not a convert and she still had deep reservations about the real motives behind their bonhomie, their kindnesses and the free-flowing alcoholic beverages. She certainly wasn't about to lower her defences, either amorous or professional, because on both counts she would be a loser. She was under no illusion who she was dealing with in spite of Giuseppe's 'big soft teddy bear' image or maybe more so because of it. To her eyes Giuseppe was a distraction, a sort of accompaniment to the main event.

Julia was refusing another Brandy when Franco's return hit her like a thunderbolt. He had shed his tie and undone the upper buttons of his snow-white shirt revealing a cluster of strands on his virile chest. She almost choked as her breath screeched to a halt on a huge knot in her throat. Then like wildfire it tore through every vein when her eyes met his, swiftly drifting to take in his broad shoulders, his muscular arms and hips and his wicked small waist. Michelangelo could not have sculpted a more perfect frame. He strode towards her with the amazing grace of a panther in full pursuit but in slow motion. That in a nutshell was Franco.

He said something to her but she failed to register a single word. She was shocked by the devastating effect he was having on her. True to tell, he was endowed with a few handsome features in his physique not least of all his slim masculinity but she hadn't until then found it that devastatingly attractive to turn her life upside down.

Before that evening, not only had she not found his arrogance, condensed in his chiselled face, particularly endearing but it was a complete turn-off. He had been insufferable at Andrea's party and she would have asked him to leave if it had been her own. How could it be that now the same roguish haughtiness she had so despised, was wreaking havoc inside her? How could she have changed so much in such a short time? She stood up to leave.

"I thought you might like to join me at Mojo's. There's a live band playing tonight. One of my part-time waiters is playing the drums and I promised I'd go."

As he spoke he casually placed his hand on the small of her back. A sharp passion scorched her like a ferocious whip giving her flushed cheeks. She was terrified and the red that rose to her cheeks made it obvious to her hosts. She couldn't even trust her own body and her self-confidence was once again torn into shreds. Her fallen gaze was somewhere between indignation and shame.

"Oh, no thank you, early start tomorrow."

She prayed Franco's hand would retreat and restore some peace and tranquillity to her shuddering body. But her prayers were in vain. So she gently pulled herself away and not wanting to sound rude pretended to address Giuseppe. She needed to retain her composure. The last thing she wanted was to show Franco he was gaining the upper hand with her. Because once she was out of there this would all be forgotten.

"Sorry if I alarmed you a little it wasn't intentional. We Italians tend to be rather tactile. It's in our Mediterranean blood, I'm afraid. I know English custom discourages such show of warmth in public. I'm sorry."

"That's alright." she improvised.

"So, won't you join me for just a little while then? We won't stay long, I promise."

"I'd love to you but I've to go."

"Will you allow me to give you a lift home then?"

"Actually there's no need for that. My car is outside."

"You can't be driving home, Julia, not with all the alcohol in your system. It'll be madness."

She knew he was right and couldn't understand why she even said that. She had never done drink and drive and should not be starting now. But deep inside she felt if she had asked to call a taxi home he would certainly offer her a ride and her suspicions were proved correct.

"I don't know why I said that. I don't normally drink and drive, honestly. I guess I wasn't expecting to stay so late, Franco, or drink so much. But thanks for a very delightful evening. I thoroughly enjoyed myself especially the Sicilian torte. I'll call a taxi if you don't mind and call for the car tomorrow with Lindsey. It's not a problem."

The dark blue flicker in Franco's eyes told her he wasn't accepting any of that.

"Julia I can drive you home, I've only had one glass", he drawled.

"No Franco I'll call a taxi."

"I can't leave you in the hands of a taxi driver at this late hour, Julia. Wait here and I'll bring my car around to the front."

Before she could reiterate her resolute words, Franco had disappeared. Giuseppe too had fled into the kitchen with untold celerity and returned brandishing a plastic bag laden with goodies. Farewells over, she found herself nestled in a comfortable front seat next to Franco. It was a cocktail of conflicting emotions churning inside her. Every nerve in her body was still reeling from the bewildering onslaught of passion.

That evening something had changed and changed dramatically. It was a fateful moment in her life because whatever it was that had changed was inside her. This wasn't something she felt would go away quickly. Incredibly, the fleeting view of Franco's majestic chest had awakened something dark and deep inside her, primeval even. It troubled her no end. That furtive look in his eyes had thrown a magnetic net around her which she knew she would find increasingly gruelling to shake off. Seated in such close proximity to him now, she didn't once dare lift her head for fear his gaunt profile might once again propel her into the unfamiliar dark place.

Chapter 3

Finally back home she breathed a huge sigh of relief. Reluctantly she had to admit, even in his car on their own, he had acted like a true gent. She had said very little even though she had so many questions she needed answers to. She made herself a cup of tea and sat in front of the telly. But she didn't watch anything. She was much too excited about how amazingly well the evening had gone to be able to concentrate on anything on the screen.

An invigorating feeling of well-being permeated her. It was an alluring feeling she was unaccustomed to and already in her mind she was envisaging great things. But she didn't want to allow her flighty imagination run out of control. It would have been inadvisably premature. So she applied the brakes and immediately her thoughts flocked back to the inimitable Giuseppe. He was such a docile and endearing father figure any girl would have loved to adopt and she wasn't any different.

Unfortunately, there was a downside. There was Franco with his predatory volitions and he wasn't going to make life easy for her. Despite the mask of bonhomie and magnanimity his azure gaze could not conceal the presence of a prowling predator. The serious suspicions she harboured about his true intentions were still standing. He was merely biding his time until the opportune moment presented itself when he would pounce and he would. But now she too had become part of the problem because she had allowed herself to be sucked into his supreme physical sway.

She turned off the telly and lumbered upstairs to her bedroom. She sat down at her dresser and stared at the tousled reflection in the mirror as she applied a thin film of moisturiser to her face. Rambling thoughts thudded inside her head and fled leaving a vacuous vale where thoughts of any kind were unwelcome. She listlessly combed her hair and then, oddly, applied a touch of lipstick and a finger-tip of eye-shadow. She was ready. But ready for what though? She was only going to bed. Intense frustration gripped her. She stood up confused but unnerved, shook her head and smiled.

Her mind was clearly playing games on her. She resented it and had to stop it there and then before she lost the plot. Wiping her face she walked up to the window. It was raining outside and under the eerie spray of street lights everything looked hazy. Sleep hadn't overcome her yet and soon enough the figure of Franco hovered in her head again. She wondered why his primal masculinity suddenly overwhelmed her feminine vulnerability so much. Was she really attracted to him? If she was, she was the last woman on earth to understand why. On a normal day Franco would not even make her list of top twenty sexiest men let alone the top ten. But then nothing seemed to be normal with her these days.

Granted, she had always found hairy chests quite enthralling especially the touch of soft down and the salty taste of the roots had always sent wild sensations storming through her blood stream. But this was ridiculous. All she had seen were a few limp strands for an insignificant number of seconds. Surely it couldn't be the sole source of this incongruous attraction. So what else could it be? His hard mouth deliberately curled into a provocative smile? His deep blue gaze intent on penetrating her soul? Or maybe his basic self-indulgence inexorably set on taming her defences and having his way with her?

Could she really find any of these unsubtle details enthralling and attractive in a man she had disliked from day one? Whatever it was that had hoodwinked her defences. The bottom line was she couldn't stop thinking of Franco and the more she allowed graphic titbits of his persona the freedom of her unguarded thoughts, the more tempestuously her pulses rocketed to the sky.

Amid all this confusion, however, her curiosity beckoned, bringing a moment of soothing relief to her being. Was Franco himself subject to this same anomaly that was haranguing her, victim to a tortuous passion the like of which he had never encountered perhaps? The thought he too might be a novice of sorts in this all-consuming jungle of turmoil allayed a swarm of fears and suspicions and rekindled her confidence and on that serene note she finally retired.

By sunrise the rain had died out completely and only sparse raindrops glittered lingeringly on the edge of some leaves. The warm fingers of the sun started to wipe them dry leaving in their wake fragrant front gardens and immaculate drives. A gloriously blithe blue sky shed a gleeful buoyant mood. She gingerly slipped into a sleek lime dress and matching shoes, combed her hair, applied light make-up, took a deep sharp breath and set off to work with a list of urgent do's in the forefront of her mind. Top of her list was a venue for her dream boutique, somewhere in Bournemouth maybe. That shouldn't be too difficult for an accomplished estate agent like her. Lindsey would no doubt want to have her say too. Then there would be some choicest items of furniture to consider for her dream shop, something substantial and stylish enough but also understated to leave the limelight to the main attraction, the shoes themselves. In her mind it seemed such a simple task but she was convinced it would be a challenge and a half especially with Lindsey chipping in at will. Thankfully, she only had a couple of appointments all day in her diary and both were in the vicinity. But before that she had to pick up the car pronto. Until she sat in Lindsey's car, she couldn't remember a day when she was happier going to work. Thankfully

Franco's figure had been brushed aside to the fringes of her thoughts. But Lindsey didn't waste a minute before she started quizzing her about the events of the previous night. She refused to believe he never made a pass at her and regretted missing out on the chance of herself meeting Franco again.

"Well, it's the truth, Lindsey. But I tell you, you've to meet his brother Giuseppe, he's the real darling."

She went on telling her about the delicious torte he made especially for her with the hope she might succeed in diverting her misplaced interest.

"Is he as good-looking as his brother?"

"I'll let you be the judge of that." Then she told her about her imminent plans to kick-start her dream hoping she would leave the Franco saga alone for a while.

"Did all this come about last night? Did Franco have anything to do with it, Julia? Come on you can tell me."

"No, Franco had nothing to do with anything. This is purely me. I think it is the right time to finally make my dream come true. You know how long I've been waiting for this moment. Maybe meeting a successful man like Franco may have provided the final thrust. But nothing more beyond that and you better believe me Lindsey."

Lindsey herself was thrilled to bits about the whole operation and hoped she could play an important part too. She said Bournemouth town centre close to the main thoroughfare would be an ideal location. She even thought she had recently seen a 'To Let' sign but couldn't remember where exactly.

They exchanged a reckless number of plans for the lay-out. Julia had looked up stuff on a designer website to spruce up her ideas, also had approached a couple of exclusive shoe stores in upmarket Knightsbridge on her last outing to London. Both had suggested a minimal approach and couldn't emphasise enough the importance of the location for the ultimate success of her business venture.

"At this early stage I obviously need to take everything on board especially advice from experts and successful entrepreneurs."

"So when do you intend to start then?" Lindsey's face could not conceal her intrinsic joy at the simple thought of such an amazing prospect.

"Today."

"Are you serious?"

"Of course I'm serious. The next step for me is to go to Italy". Her voice purred as the pupils of her eyes lit up her face. "I need to go and see for myself their most exclusive shoe stores where the rich and famous of this world purchase their exclusive footwear. I want to see with my own eyes how they set up their stores, how they use the space and props and lighting. I want to get everything right, to the slightest detail. With celebrity clients nothing must be taken for granted and every bit of subtlety counts. I have to know how servicing the rich and powerful works. I don't want to panic every time Penelope Cruz or Julia Roberts walked in." She laughed candidly simulating in her mind having coffee with Meryl Streep while she lovingly cuddled one of her exclusive items.

Lindsey grimaced momentarily.

"Don't you think you might be jumping the gun a little bit? Won't it be wiser to take things more gently?"

"Lindsey, don't worry, my head is in the right place."

"It's not going to be as easy as you make it sound, is it really?"

"Why can't you just be happy for me?" Her frustration was furrowed on her forehead. It had been the happiest morning for a long while and the last thing she had expected was someone, least of all Lindsey, to put a damper on her enthusiasm.

"I've got it all planned up here, Lindsey, what could go wrong?"

"I don't know, Julia. It's not that I'm not happy, you know I am. I just don't want you to let your imagination run away with you. Raising your expectations too high is dangerous. If things don't work out the way you plan then it'll hurt and may have serious repercussions. You don't have the experience to jump into something big like this with your eyes closed."

"Lindsey, my eyes aren't closed, nor is my mind. That's why I want to go to Italy, the homeland of designer footwear. I want to learn from the experts."

"I suppose you're entitled to make your dream come true and take risks."

"Yes, I've been planning this all my life. Be positive Lindsey and wish me well."

"You're right. I'm sorry. You know I'm behind you all the way. Honestly. I just want you to be careful, that's all." She paused briefly, looked at her and pursed her lips in apprehension.

Later on, when Julia returned from her first appointment they popped out for a quick coffee. It being an exceptionally sunny day, several tables were laid out on the terrace outside the coffee bar. They sat down and ordered a Cappuccino and a café-latte with a brace of mini-donuts. Before long the conversation turned to Franco once more. Lindsey was convinced Franco must have had a finger in the pie because this was very uncharacteristic of her best friend.

Julia reluctantly broached the subject unable to quench Lindsey's endemic curiosity. She wanted to know everything, every word that was said, every item consumed apart from the special Italian torte, who sat next to who, even the time Julia eventually arrived home.

"Did Franco come in for a coffee?"

"No. Certainly not," she promptly yelled annoyed and almost insulted by the sassiness of the question.

"Well he wanted to but I declined," she said lying through her teeth trying to relax the tone of their exchanges.

"You didn't, did you? Are you serious Julia?" she sniggered.

"Lindsey, why would I want to lie to you?" She deliberately dwelt on every syllable. Then promptly she went on.

"Actually it's a lie. He never asked and I didn't want him to either."

Lindsey shook her head. The annoyance in her eyes spelled in no uncertain terms that in her opinion Julia had missed a huge opportunity. But before she could say anything she noticed Julia's lips harden and her eyes were about to shoot daggers at her. So she kept the peace and chewed her donut.

"Speaking of the devil," eyebrows fully arched she turned her head towards a distant silhouette. Julia initially frowned confounded by the sudden effusion of colour on Lindsey's face. She turned as her narrowed eyes scanned the variegated stream of day-trippers. But her heart sank even before her eyes fell on those of the approaching devil. Her mouth dried up and her throat scorched. She couldn't even swallow. "Hello ladies."

Franco was still a good ten yards away so heads turned from other tables too.

"May I join you?" It was a deep measured voice that transfixed her gaze. His wide shoulders loomed above her tightly clamped in a snow white shirt, immaculately pressed with the customary top button undone. She could not risk looking at his chest not for a single second because she knew the devastating effect it would have on her. The last thing she needed at that moment was to leak signals revealing her crumbling defences.

"And now that I've joined you", his jet black brows lifted, "will you join me for another coffee or maybe something stiffer?"

He leaned back in his chair intimating time was on his side. He watched Julia intently with eyes that would not entertain a negative response. She felt obliged to speak first despite the harrowing tension beating inside. She hoped her voice would drown her turmoil and sound normal.

"Well, in that case another *latte* please."

Her eyes veered towards Lindsey expectantly. He must have followed them from the car park, she thought. But Lindsey deliberately evaded her glance and casually checked the time on her watch. Then she suddenly stumbled to her feet, excused herself profusely, gave them both a polite kiss on the cheek and took her leave. Julia was horrified by the flat savage behaviour of her friend. How could she leave her so defenceless? Surely she could have easily concocted an apt excuse for both of them. She had done it so often before without the slightest effort. Why not this time?

How on earth was she going to disentangle herself from this terrifying knot without making an undignified exit? What could she possibly say which wouldn't sound ungrateful?

Sensing the awkwardness suddenly hounding Julia, Franco stood up and made a suggestion.

"In that case, Julia, let me buy you lunch. There's a nice little Thai restaurant not far from here. It's a jewel, believe me."

She was even more shocked by this latest offer, but having no plausible excuse at the ready, she thought it wiser to accept. As she walked beside him it was an overwhelming relief to be free from his glinting scrutiny and from the view of his terrifying chest. Each time he turned to speak to her she lowered her gaze evasively. But as she listened she braced herself for what was going to be a difficult afternoon.

"It's a glorious day isn't it?" she said inanely.

"Yes, it's perfect for a table for two out on the terrace. You're going to love this restaurant."

When they sat down on the edge of the hillside with the expansive Cornish coast in all its sun-kissed beauty unfolding below them, she relaxed a little. She allowed him to choose for her.

Hovering over the glossy menu, he shrugged, picked a light banquet for two and asked for the wine list. But it was a mere formality for as soon as the wine list arrived he only glanced at it for a brief second then ordered a bottle of Château Margaux.

"So," It was the voice of the tempter, that same voice he had used the previous night when he offered her a lift home. But she had prevailed then and would do so again. She was much calmer now keeping her eyes level trying to stay aloof of the snare she was convinced lurked behind his engaging gaze.

The Thai delicacies were divine. They regaled her taste buds to a rare feast of aromas, nuances and exquisite culinary delights. But the exceptional bottle of Bordeaux's finest was the crown of the quasi-orgasmic ritual. So much so she completely neglected her defences, sitting vulnerably at the mercy of the extraordinary mix of ambrosia, nectar and charm.

"So, you didn't tell me much about your dream boutique last night?" It was a matter-of-fact question to salvage an ailing conversation.

" I tend to remember you had an important call just when I was about to tell you."

"Oh, I'm sorry about that," he shrugged. "Well, here I am now and my mobile is switched off. I'll be delighted to hear what you're dreaming of."

"I haven't started anything yet. At the moment it's just an idea."

"I'm glad about that. I wouldn't want you to make any expensive mistakes at the outset," he said nonchalantly, raising his glass to his mouth. "Isn't this wine something else? And it's not quite its best year you know. Nowhere near. Nevertheless it's a bouquet you don't easily forget."

"Yes, it's exceptionally delicious."

The waiter approached, smiled politely, asked if the food was to their satisfaction, deftly topped their glasses and walked away.

"No point wasting it." He took another sip. "Well, opening a fashion outlet these days is a cut-throat business, you must know that. And you've to research to see if there is sufficient customer demand for the products you're offering."

"My plan is to open a very exclusive women's shoe store with celebrity clients in mind, top of the range footwear mainly and perhaps handbags from Italy."

"Ah, I see the young lady has a commendable taste for those admirably rare commodities only the rich and famous can ever enjoy." His mouth hardened.

"That's exactly why I chose this place. It has class written all over it."

Julia couldn't quite see the connection he was making. What common ground could there be between a Thai restaurant and an Italian shoe store? Except for the discerning clients who might frequent both establishments, her thoughts jangled. What other comparisons could one make between spring rolls and stilettos?

"You see, you can learn a lot by coming to a place like this which may not be readily obvious to the average customer. But irrespective of what your main product is, be it food, shoes, cars, what matters infinitely more these days to the customer is the quality and honesty of the service, the authenticity of your establishment. It's the only way you can guarantee customers will come back again and again."

"I understand service matters… " Julia managed to squeeze in.

"Julia, in this restaurant they believe in strict discipline and everything is genuine. Their service is paramount to them and to us. You can stroll into the kitchen anytime and I promise you, you won't find a single fault with it. Their code of cleanliness is unequalled. And I know because it is my business to know these things."

"So I take it your kitchen too enjoys these admirably high standards, then." she teased tentatively.

Transfixed on his glass of wine he dismissed her gratuitous jibe without even a smile or grimace. Then for a long moment he held her gaze with a chilling reserve sending a cold shiver down her spine. She picked up her glass to soothe her jangled nerves. She was starting to feel uncomfortable.

"I believe so. And where to now?" he said curtly.

She wasn't quite sure what he meant. She warily considered the austere lines on his face.

"I don't mean where you're going now, that's none of my business", he went on reading perfectly well the confusion mapped out on her face.

She suspected he could probably tell what she was thinking just by delving into her eyes. Caution spiralled inside her once again. Here she was sitting with this formidable man always in control, unflappable and a master of strategy. She should never forget, especially when under the influence of a remarkable bottle of Bordeaux. He was a complex giant of a man, a redoubtable man but one to be admired too, she reluctantly conceded to herself.

"I mean your shoe store, Julia. Any specific location, brand range, image, advertising and target celebrity confraternity, if any? I'll promise to provide the Champagne for the grand opening."

"Oh, I haven't got that far yet. But I'm sure Lindsey will help me."

She couldn't think of anything more apt to say at that moment, the wine managed to comatose every cell in her brain, numbing every limb in her body which was now craving a lulling siesta.

"But I know I want to open in Bournemouth town centre."

"Bournemouth, I like Bournemouth." Realising he caught her on the wrong foot, he skilfully steered the conversation to other cursory matters.

"Lindsey can be an awkward customer sometimes", she honestly confessed, red in the face. "But she's always been there for me, you know. She's worth every one of her in gold."

"True friends normally are but I take it she's not a career woman", he paused, resting his gaze exclusively on her, "like you."

His words were simple but crisp. They instantly stirred something ferocious inside her, impeding her breath. He smiled revealing a set of perfect teeth which lit up his face more than the shimmering sunshine.

"Have you ever been married?"

"No", she said, wondering where the conversation was going. Her eyes lingered momentarily on his slim tanned neck but as the black wisp on his chest hit her gaze, her heart sank and her defences simply crumbled. A reckless impulse was compelling her to run her tongue over his chest and taste the salty cocktail, run her fingers over his beautiful lips and kiss them. A rush of blood burned her cheeks. Her limbs were still numb. She was tempted to ask him the same question but then something in her head, stopped her. She couldn't allow herself to carelessly divulge a shred of interest in him because the simple truth was there wasn't any.

Why had he not made a pass at her the previous night, when they were all alone in his car, she suddenly wondered for no particular reason?

"Why do you ask?" Her tone was hoarse and tentative.

"You're a very beautiful woman, Julia, and I'm sure I'm not the first man to have popped that question to you." His eyes fixed on her lips he smiled cynically half-expecting an equally cynical reply. But seeing his pert remark did not elicit a reaction he went on.

"Is that because the right Knight in shining armour hasn't yet come along?"

The music in his voice was intoxicating. Not only had he broken through her defences with the greatest ease but incredibly the physical attraction had grown into an obsession and all she wanted from him was to carry her in his strong arms, make sweet love to her and turn her unbearable torture into an ecstatic explosion of screaming sensations. A sea of lust engulfed her and she floated helplessly like a rudderless boat. If he decided to leave now she would not even have the strength to stand let alone walk. Was he aware of the havoc he had wreaked inside her?

"Julia." he firmly said. She was transfixed by his mouth. "I like you. I really do and I want you."

Before she could string together a few apt words to pour cold water on his ardour, he leant across the table, gently ran his hand over the column of her neck, pulled her firmly closer and nibbled at her lower lip. A volcano of emotions ripped through her, she was so far gone she just wanted more and more. Her heart stopped beating while his hand teased the small of her back and his tongue explored her mouth. His face was taut with extreme hunger, his eyes oozing pleasure.

Her hand, still shuddering from the shock reached out and rested on his cheek. She then ran her fingers through his glossy hair.

"God, I want you Julia". His heavy voice creaked. She could hardly breathe as his mouth devoured hers once again. Her heart leapt in ecstasy, her pulse raced erratically and a deluge of pleasure surged through every nerve and every limb. Only then did she realise what she had been missing, how in a few fleeting moments the hollow inside her was bursting with joy. Only then did she realise how much she really needed this.

A young couple walking past them glanced wistfully. Through the corner of her eye Julia caught their shadow and instantly backed off in a panic.

"What is it, Julia? We haven't done anything wrong, you know. We just kissed. An ordinary couple who like each other normally do."

But that was it, they weren't an ordinary couple. In fact, they weren't anything at all. This was a huge mistake and Lindsey carried most of the blame. She should have found some limp excuse too and made her escape with her. So what now?

"What are you're doing this afternoon?" The gleam in his eyes grew as he held her gaze.

"I've to go. There's so much to do. Thanks for lunch." Her voice was weak and husky.

"Julia, I wasn't inviting you for sex. I'm not a player. I seriously think we've got something here. I could see the way you responded to me. And my body loves you. The chemistry is perfect."

"I don't think so", she lied. Her anger clung to her. She refused to raise his hopes and desperately tried not to look at him but it was a battle she couldn't win. She was far too intoxicated by his tanned masculinity and the knot of chest hair that tormented her endlessly.

"Look. I'm sorry if you got the wrong idea but I don't need this. I can't do this."

He raised an eyebrow and a broad smile settled on his rose lips.

"Look." he said calmly. "If the fact that I like you scares you, I can't really change that. I can't help it." He chewed his lips while he contemplated her.

She shuddered unable to fight the magnetism drawing her towards him.

"But I don't understand why you're afraid of me."

"I'm not afraid of you, Franco." she rasped, completely taken aback by the sudden rush of adrenaline coming to her rescue from absolutely nowhere. "Truly, I'm not." Her voice had regained a new-fangled fervour which started to calm her nerves and relaxed her taut cheeks.

"Then what is it? Was my kiss distasteful? It didn't seem to be the case from where I was sitting."

His swift jab found no ready response from her. She could not lie as there were witnesses to the peaks of pleasure that had entranced her body.

"Franco, I don't need this now. I've plans of my own and I'm not going to let this moment of madness ruin everything. I've waited a lifetime to see my dream become a reality. I'm sorry." At this stage her fragile voice almost cracked.

"Moment of madness, you say." He spoke casually but firmly. "Not for me. More like the moment of truth. But, fine. I respect your wish for now. Then let me help you with your plans. Let's not part on opposite sides. Whether you like it or not, we can be just friends. Julia, I like you as a person. I really do. And I'm not going to walk away."

As she looked at him she fought the tears. Kiss me again she wanted to scream, as a ravenous hunger pierced her stomach. She stood up pretending to leave but before she took the first step Franco pulled her into his arms and kissed her forehead, then her eyelids and finally his scorched mouth found hers. Her world that was about to collapse only a few minutes earlier was now basking in soothing warmth.

"I can help you make your dream come true." It was the last thing she wanted to hear.

Chapter 4

Her flight from London Heathrow was pleasant and she hardly had time to get overly excited about it when the plane landed in Milan. As soon as she got to her hotel she picked up her room key, dumped her luggage and before she knew it she was sitting in her taxi hurtling down the Via Nazzionale. It was just after two when she stepped out into the glorious sunlight in the very heart of Europe's exclusive shoppers' paradise.

Shop-windows glistened as groups of smartly-clad shoppers bustled up and down the street, hopping in and out carrying oversize designer bags. She took a deep breath and climbed the few steps leading into what seemed like the most popular fashion outlet. There was electricity in the air and for a moment she felt like a guest model on a celebrity catwalk. An array of colourful skirts, tops, dresses and men's suits whizzed past her on either side walking along the fashion houses in the Galleria. Much impressed as she was, reluctantly she turned around and walked out into the scorching heat again.

She sailed along, a latter day Alice in Wonderland, taking brief notes at regular intervals. Occasionally shutting her eyes she tried to imagine her own outlet maybe one day in Milan too. Her opening night would make a centre page pull-out in the local papers with bevies of photographers, journalists, business big shots from the Chamber of Commerce, local celebrities from radio, television and entertainment, the whole gamut of Who's Who of personalities.

She stepped into *"Creazioni Silvano"* and spotted a striking collection of Cormelia shoes. They oozed elegance and a refreshing originality of design. She tried on a red pair which blew her away. But she wasn't going to rush into buying or ordering anything on the first day. Her education had only just begun. She scratched her chin and strolled next door to *"Moda Donna"*, an exclusive house for top of the range handbags. The variety was incredible. But so was their price.

Just outside the galleria, dwarfed by the colossal *Duomo* looming in the centre of the square, a modest store peered at her. Most shoppers walked briskly by. But Julia was looking for good deals and she knew from her University days, sometimes the more modest and the less glowing stores too could be the keepers of precious little gems.

"Stivali?" asked Julia.

"Sí, Signorina.?" The man in a black shirt and a matching charcoal suit, probably in his mid-forties, smiled and welcomed her. Incredibly, he had an uncanny likeness to Franco. He could have easily been a lost twin brother, she thought.

"We do a vast range of ladies boots here. We've just received some nice *Stivaletti t*oo."

"*Stivaletti?*"

"They're short boots, below the knees, *Signorina*."

He brought out box after box, each pair more striking and more gorgeous than the previous one. Julia kept her cool but promised she would return. Across the square there was another fashion heaven. It was called:

"*Scarpe di Lusso*". It was packed to the rafters with class and elegance and a carnival of styles and colours. What a joy it was holding them in her hands and trying them on. But one particular pair of beige *stivaletti* caught her eye. They were divine. What really set them apart was a Swarovski crystal embedded in the ankle strap. She could not take her eyes off them. She put them on and paid for them. Then she asked for a bag for her own shoes and while they wrapped them up she asked a few questions too about bulk buying and major shoe factories in Milan.

"I'm sure you'll see me again", she said.

"*Sarà un grande piacere, Signorina.*"

The rest of the day flitted past her like a flash. She spent most of the evening in her room, talking to herself and to her new boots, delving into the pages of the magazines she had picked up.

The next day went by as quickly and was even more thrilling than the first. She could really get used to this leisurely lifestyle and was quickly becoming enamoured of the idea of opening a plush outlet in Milan. That new sparkle in her eyes made her even more determined to make a success of her Bournemouth store, her stepping stone to a more eminent status. She wasn't going to be side-tracked by anything or anyone.

That night instead of staying in her hotel room reading and watching some Italian chat show she ventured into Milan's chic night life. Her first point of call was a quiet little Bistro, La Trattoria. There were only two other couples sharing an intimate moment over pizza and wine. The décor was warm and simple. It lifted her spirit just being there, away from the hustle and bustle of her normal life, free to move around at will, surrounded by people who smiled most of their waking hours. These were happy people who evidently enjoyed their jobs, their life and their food. Milan was a happy place. She could live there alright. It would be one of the easiest decisions of her life.

She ordered a plate of pasta "*alla puttana*" and a chilled glass of Pinot Grigio. She cast a fleeting glance around her and wondered why such an elegant, top drawer establishment was so quiet. The two tall barmen chatted lazily.

"Signorina, we Italians like to eat a little later," the bespectacled waiter said. "It gets busier in an hour or two." His eyes discreetly surveyed her curves as he placed a few olives, garlic bread and the glass of wine on her table.

"Buona Sera, Signorina." a dark voice rasped behind her.

It was not an unfamiliar voice but she was a complete stranger to everyone here. She turned in a slight shrug as a cold shiver ran down her spine.

"Julia." It was a heavy, sensuous wail this time, more familiar and more terrifying. He stood in front of her, shiny black hair combed back, immaculate black shirt and pressed black trousers. A polished set of white teeth smiled at her as his Mediterranean gaze roved her all over, finally settling on her troubled green eyes.

"I see you're very single tonight." A slight taunt in his eyes choked her.

"Franco." Her mouth eased into a polite smile but her voice croaked feebly. For a moment she didn't know what to say or do. She sat sheepishly, angry at the embarrassing blushes invading her cheeks.

"So, how are you? I didn't know Milan was one of your favourite hangouts."

His measured sardonic tones grabbed her like a tight clamp and his raised dark brows on his placid face did not make it any easier.

"It's just a short break." she heard herself say, doggedly.

It made her indecision even more frustrating.

"May I join you?"

Before she had time to overcome her initial shock he had sat down next to her and called the spectacled waiter for a Scotch and tonic.

"I'm not really hungry tonight", he went on. "People like me who basically live with food tend to learn very quickly that less is more."

"Oh." She said lamely. She struggled within herself to keep him at bay. She hoped she could hold sway over the conversation and more importantly over her own unpredictable nerves. She had to quell the growing unrest inside her. The mere sight of him and the sound of his voice had made her nerve ends hysterical. Her hands were damp. She could sense that every word she said would conspire to embarrass her. But she wasn't going to get up and leave him sitting by himself. That much she knew. It would have been much too uncouth and ungrateful. After all, he'd only been civil and graceful to her.

"Has your friend not come with you then?"

"Oh Lindsey, you mean?" Realising that she was the only friend known to Franco she went on. "No, I'm here on my own for a short break. Just to recharge the batteries and do a bit of window shopping."

"Good, everyone needs some personal space and time." Franco's eyes teased and nuzzled at her lean neck while a swaggering smile settled on his lips. "So, how long is your short break?"

"Just the week."

"Julia, you haven't a young Milanese lover by any chance, have you? Has he stood you up tonight?"

The shocking arrogance of the man angered and mortified her. Yet her eyes clung to his taunting sneer as if he had just paid her a compliment. She picked up her glass and took a long sip to lubricate her parched tongue.

"No, there is no lover at all in Milan or anywhere else, I'll have you know." Her eyes cast a dark shadow over her face. "I'm just having a quiet evening tonight. Why do you find that so hard to accept?"

"Well in Milan you don't see too many beautiful girls like you dining alone." A beguiling frown beckoned. He pressed his lips together and shook his head, rather patronisingly. "I know in the U.K. no one butts an eyelid. But in Milan, not cool. Not cool at all. He paused, turning to the waiter standing at the entrance.

"You know, meeting you here, I'm building an appetite. I think I'll have a pizza if you don't mind. They make good pizzas here."

Julia was simply flabbergasted. He went ahead and ordered his pizza and a bottle of chilled *Verdicchio* with two glasses. Her breath became more audible and the disturbed stillness made her pulse more erratic. She was suddenly a prey to an uncontrollable surge of heat in her bloodstream and it scared her.

How was she going to survive the rest of the evening alone with him? If only she had asked Lindsey to come with her? If only she hadn't been so complacent and single-minded. A string of doubts tormented her making her ever more edgy. She was convinced that soon the conversation would turn to that fateful kiss back in Poole. Once more she would be at his mercy. Unless Lindsey suddenly staggered breezily into the *Trattoria* like Wonder Woman and whisked her away to a distant haven far from the imminent danger.

But as the minutes wore on, her edginess gave way to a measured confidence and she gradually relaxed.

"I take it you didn't like me very much the first time you saw me?"

After an awkward long pause, Julia shook her head, eyes fastened to the tablecloth.

"Well, the straight answer is no, I didn't. I dislike brash arrogance, full stop, especially in men. It's a complete turn-off to me."

He looked at her without a flicker of an eyelid.

"Complete turn-off. Well, I knew I hadn't exactly charmed you to bits. But hey, I've always loved the limelight. And I think you love it too because your future seems that way inclined."

He smiled at the knowledge she had warmed to him since their first meeting. His azure eyes teased her, desperately trying to connect with hers. She looked austere for a moment, unnerved by his self-assured tone. She kept telling herself he was just a distraction and a complete stranger. What did she know about him anyway? Not much. She hadn't asked him about his previous conquests and she wasn't going to. But she was convinced from what she had seen so far that he'd broken a few hearts and she had no intention of adding her name to the list of crushed girlfriends.

Yet now, sitting next to him, she was feeling pins and needles in her legs. Every time their eyes met her confidence plunged and her breathing became heavier. The *Verdicchio* arrived and the waiter gracefully filled their glasses. She took a mouthful hoping it would cover up the growing disarray inside her. She looked his way but to no avail. Her whole body was caught in a red-hot clamp. She could hardly breathe.

"Will you excuse me please, Franco? I need to go to the ladies."

Her legs were still numb but somehow she managed to maintain her balance and composure. She picked up her handbag and carefully inched away not quite sure where the ladies toilets were. It was a minor problem the bespectacled waiter was happy to oblige. As for her other enormous problem it was going to take something much, much stronger than a young waiter to solve.

What was she going to do? What could she do? Now she knew for a fact the moment she relaxed her resistance, his powerful sway would devour her. She just couldn't resist him. It mystified her, angered her even. He did something to her she couldn't even explain. She felt so helpless in a foreign country where she'd come to start building her modest empire and hopefully turn her dream into something tangible and real. The timing of this impossible encounter was all wrong. She wasn't ready. Surely she'd know if she was. So why was she responding so capriciously to every word he said, every smile and every flicker of his eyelids? What was happening to her?

Franco seemed to be in control of her every limb, her every muscle and the conflicting emotions inside her. How could she have thought her defences were reliable and unassailable? The simple truth was she had never felt more vulnerable in her whole life. She had well and truly fallen under his spell.

She touched her makeup, put on another coat of lipstick and braced herself as she returned to her table.

"I'm sorry, Franco, I'm not feeling too good. You'll have to excuse me."

She drew the attention of the bespectacled waiter and asked for a taxi and her bill. But

Franco had already figured out a congenial alternative. He had settled the bill and was brandishing a set of keys.

"Don't be silly, Julia. It would be very ill-mannered of me to let you take a taxi at this hour."

"Honestly, it's quite alright, Franco. I'll be fine. And thanks for picking up the bill but you shouldn't have."

"Pleasure, Julia. But I'm not taking no for an answer." He diplomatically dismissed the waiter.

"Come on, I'll drive you to your hotel. It's the least I can do."

She couldn't believe she was sitting in his Porsche a few seconds later, only inches away from him. She hated herself for being so incredibly weak. Never in a thousand years should she have taken up his offer. But arguing in the middle of the restaurant would only have made things worse. What she should have really done was say a polite goodnight and call a taxi herself. However, now it was too late for that. She was where she was. Her only weapon had to be silence in the car, a pithy thank you outside her hotel, no hugs or kisses.

"So, where are you staying?"

She surveyed his profile from the corner of her eyes. The measured savagery of his tone was softened by an impish twist of his full lips. For a long moment she stood her ground and said nothing.

"Julia, I don't intend to drive around Milan in circles all night. I've to drop you somewhere. Will you stop behaving like a little girl and tell me the name of your hotel."

There was no sting in his voice just slight impatience beneath the cool veneer. Maybe he should have let her take a taxi. He could sense this was turning into a churlish affair. Yet he had no intention of being boorish. There was only light traffic on the roads and he was more than happy to take her on a tour of Milan by night, until she decided to reveal the name of her mystery hotel. Sooner or later she would have to.

"Is it the Renaissance, The Hilton or the Palazzo?"

She evasively surveyed the tall palms lining the avenue with military constancy. She could have done with a Vodka and coke. Her nerves were starting to fray. Swallowing awkwardly she tried to sit up more comfortably in her seat. She looked straight ahead of her but unfailingly sensed his wide shoulders lifting and his grip on the steering-wheel relaxing.

"Julia, what do I have to do to show you that I'm genuinely fond of you? You must know it by now. I really like you. Have I done anything to deserve this chilly treatment? Why do you dislike me so much? Won't you tell me?"

Deep and intense desolation shook the roots of her entrails. Somehow she managed to hold on to her diplomatic silence. Her head was heavy and her eyelids too. The hypnotising sway which engulfed her terrified her.

"I don't." It was hardly a whisper.

He shrugged not sure whether he'd heard correctly. But if what he had heard was indeed correct then he did not want to undermine her sensitivity with a barrage of soul-searching questions. His narrowed eyes contemplated her, hoping dearly he could soften her pig-headedness. He found her so irresistible when she was tense and cross. It was an overwhelming relief to have heard her voice, albeit a mere whisper. He swiftly thought of something delicate to say to her before silence chilled the atmosphere again.

"Thank you, Julia."

They were soave words that purred to her heart. She closed her eyes finding the honesty of the moment disarming. She was afraid to reopen them but reopen them she did and instantly the bitter bleakness in her heart rose like a morning mist. She sighed keeping her eyes level and calm. The silence that had crackled with tension was now raw with emotion.

It would have given Franco an incalculable lift if she had whispered another word or two. But the tension was getting to him too.

"Well, if you won't tell me the name of your hotel", he said impishly, "it leaves me no other option."

Horrified, she instantly wondered what the option might be. But she wasn't given much time to figure out as he veered into a quaint country lane, up a steep hill to a sedate stop in front of a delightfully illuminated white villa. He jumped out and walked to her door, opened it and waited.

"What you're doing?" Her frown hit him like a brick. "If you think I'm sleeping with you, you've got something else coming, Franco. How dare you bring me here? Take me to my hotel before I scream."

"Julia, I can't read your mind, I tried to take you to your hotel but you wouldn't tell me where you're staying. What was I to do? Did you really think I'd leave you in the hands of a stranger in a taxi at this hour? Or drop you in the middle of nowhere? I couldn't do it my worst enemy."

Her stomach churned as Franco held her gaze. It was a chilling moment which took a long way to convince her, if indeed she needed more convincing, of his upright intentions. But she had never thought of him as having enemies despite his brash demeanour.

"That's not the way my granny brought me up."

"Granny?" she heard herself croak.

"Yes, my granny. My mother died at my birth." he paused. "I guess, you could say I killed her." His austere face refused to smile at what sounded like a misplaced joke. "But that was many years ago and my suspended sentence still hangs over me. There, now you know."

Her defiant frown intimated she wasn't going to soften out of sympathy for his distant misfortune. So, his mother had died. These things happen. Her Dad had walked out on her and her Mum when she was nine but she wasn't about to use that as a cheap tactic.

"Look, Julia, I didn't bring you here so I could pressure you into sleeping with me. If you had given me a chance, you would be in your hotel by now. But we're here and at least we're talking like adults. So, why don't you get out of the car, come and have a cup of coffee or something and we can talk in a civil way in my lounge. Don't worry I've four bedrooms and a great big Labrador who'll protect you from me."

As Julia sat in his sleek, soft-hued lounge caution spiralled through her. Had she just been plunged into the middle of an uncanny dream, she wondered, with her eyes wide open? Nothing made any sense to her anymore, who she was, where she was, why. She felt like an orphan helplessly looking up, unable to recognize anyone or anything familiar to lift her heart. An eerie cluster of dark emotions filled her being with rage, remorse, regret and distress.

When Franco returned with her large mug of tea and a tray stacked with a golden mountain of *Ferrero Rocher* a sense of relief filled her lungs and tension oozed out of her stiff limbs. He poured a small whiskey and sat down opposite her.

"By the way Julia, you can have my main guest room downstairs and I'm sure Fred", pointing at the lovely black Labrador lying beside her, "would be delighted to sleep at the foot of your bed. Don't worry, my room is upstairs."

"Do I get a key to the guest room then?"

"You'll find the key inside the lock."

His bemused smile betrayed a shadow of disappointment. But then he knew trust, like the eternal city of Rome couldn't be built in a day. He wasn't naïve. At least her icy reserve had started to gently thaw. It was the most important thing for him at that moment. Trust would grow as the relationship grew, he was sure of it. But first and foremost she needed to feel more at ease with herself in his presence. He had to stop overwhelming her every time he opened his mouth or looked into her eyes.

However, the inevitable truth was that his glowing sexual aura had overwhelmed her the very first time he had laid his eyes on her. Since then she had found him even more devastatingly mesmerising the closer he got to her. That was the very nature of the beast. Attraction and sexual fascination did not seem to conform to any social norms.

"Franco, let me make one thing clear. Just because I'm using your guest room tonight does not mean anything has changed between you and me. I thought I'd better make that clear from the start."

Her stern eyes watched his mouth harden. He deliberately pursed his lips and dispatched a brooding glint.

"The lady does not mince her words. Julia, I wouldn't want it any other way. God help me if you ever thought I had taken advantage of you. You know I couldn't live with that."

The tea had managed to soothe her nerves and help generate conversation. Words started to flow more liberally and less guardedly. Every word that left their lips prompted in the other a deep-seated delight normally bestowed by unexpected gifts. Julia soon discovered they had quite a bit in common. Though their upbringing and their views on politics and religion diverged significantly, their ambitions and single-handedness drew mutual admiration.

"Would you care for a small whiskey before you retire?" He tottered across to a tray laden with an array of shimmering crystal decanters.

She thought fuzzily and made a move to get up. This was the seducing voice of a tempter and another devious way to pressure her into lowering her defences. Then he could entice her to his own bedroom or sneak into hers behind her. The thought of it alone sent a rush of blood through her body. But she had made it abundantly clear what her intentions were and so had he.

"Just a little one to help you sleep well, tea can keep you awake, you know."

Before she knew it he handed her a glass of whiskey.

"Club Soda or water with it?" he asked. "

He seemed a little alarmed by the suddenness of her query.

"Well, quite a few years now but I've hardly lived in it. I've had friends from England stay here in the past. One of them is a painter who loves it immensely. He sits on the roof and spends hours staring in the distance and at, well, I shouldn't really."

Sounding a little embarrassed she said: "Some coke then please."

He disappeared into the kitchen and returned holding a can of coke in one hand and a glass full of ice-cubes in the other. She helped herself to a couple of cubes and settled again comfortably on the cream leather sofa. If she hadn't tortured herself so much it would probably have turned into an enjoyable evening. But maybe she should have declined the alcoholic beverage and retired to the guest room assigned to her for the night. That way she would have made sure she wouldn't make any more mistakes. It was bad enough spending the night in Franco's villa. How was she going to sleep peacefully in the knowledge of his room being a few feet away from her own? More importantly, would she ever be able to forgive herself if anything happened?

Something in his serene sapphire gaze soothed her suspicions and she started to breathe less warily.

He stood up and walked to a large painting depicting a wonderful country view.

"You see this? Tomorrow you will see this same view from the balcony. Then tell me which is the better picture, this or the one outside." He paused, considered the painting for a long minute and turned to her.

"Would you've believed me if I told you it was the work of my own hands?"

She found his mocking tone quite refreshing. She allowed herself to think of him as being a very interesting man with an equally intriguing history. Undoubtedly a bright, ambitious future ahead of him littered with successes.

"Well executed," she confessed to him.

So, how long have you had the villa for?"

"Eh, I've had it for about twelve years now. When grandma died we inherited a generous windfall of cash and I never knew what to do with it." His mouth hardened. "I felt guilty for a long time thinking she hadn't spent it on herself because of us." His voice sank a little but his hazel gaze oozed a warm, passionate tenderness setting off little sparks and butterflies inside her. "But she loved this area, you know. We lived in Bergamo. She used to bring me here some weekends and used to tell me if I was ever to meet God, this was where I would find him and nowhere else. She was right, you know. I didn't really believe her at first but the idea slowly grew on me. Eventually when I didn't need any more convincing I built it for her, like a little sanctuary in her sweet memory."

He stood up, vanished into his study and came back brandishing a fading picture of his grandmother in her prime. She can't have been older than thirty.

"Her name was Maria. She was a beautiful woman. And she was even more beautiful inside." His deep love for his lovely granny glistened supremely in his blue eyes. "My grandfather was a very lucky man", emotion swamped his voice, "but I never got to know him. Unfortunately he passed away rather young, killed in the war."

"Oh, how sad I'm sorry."

"She deserved better. But, you know something, I can't remember a day there wasn't a smile on her face. She was a very happy woman in spite of everything."

He held her gaze as he spoke and she could discern genuine sorrow in his darkened, azure eyes. This was a formidable man, complex but formidable. So caught up was she in his history and his anecdotes that her defences were no longer an important issue. She had forgotten this was the same man who had more or less deviously marshalled her into accepting a risky and insane offer of a lift home. Then more outrageously cajoled her to his own remote villa.

But now that faded into insignificance. This could have been a holy man of the cloth extolling rare human virtues. She truly was in her element. Not only did she feel so much at ease now but she was lulled by every word that left his luscious pink lips. She looked at him blankly eager to hear more. He too gazed at her expectantly as a comfortable silence announced itself, a silence which amorous couples indulged in to revel in their object of desire, absorb one another allowing emotions to enthral their bodies.

"I guess she was like a mother to you." Her voice was cool, crisp.

"Yes, she was, very much so. I know no one can replace your Mum but she was the closest thing. I loved her very much. Still do."

Settling back in his couch, he sipped his whiskey and for a few seconds contemplated the picture. Then he turned and placed it on a mahogany side table, next to the phone. His neat profile was a work of art and it was then when she noticed a little dimple taking her completely by surprise.

Something primitive inside her unfurled and she started to breathe more sharply. She bit her lower lip and starkly felt a sudden impulse to nibble his lower lip too. She wanted to jump across to his sofa, lie on top of him and in her naked glory press her body close to his, her hungry lips glued to his lips. She just longed to make love to him and regale her body with a sea of orgasmic shockwaves she knew his awesome body could arouse in her.

He noticed new colour invading her cheekbones. He didn't want to react too swiftly. Self-discipline was always enviable but in this case it was indispensable. It had been a difficult and uphill battle all evening and luck had started to smile on him. He had come a long way from the previous snubs and rebuttals. He wasn't going to allow any impulsive move spoil it all now. Time was no object. If previous experience with women had taught him anything, he knew if he was ever going to get anywhere with her, he needed to be firm but gentle, available and charming but patient and reserved, close but not too close, warm and loving but equally strong and above all in control. It was simple but he had to play his cards right. He knew she wasn't an easy catch and he didn't want the obvious gains he had made that night to ebb into nothingness.

"Have you got any pictures of yourself as a young boy?"

"Let me see," He cupped his chin, pursed his sensuous lips and nodded gently.

"Yes, of course. But, I'm not sure if I've any here." Then he tapped the air with his forefinger:

"Wait a minute. I might have a few upstairs. Help yourself to some more drinks."

He disappeared upstairs closely followed by Fred and a few moments later returned smiling regally and holding a large white envelope in his hand, Fred again following closely behind.

"These were taken by my granny, many moons ago." His face glowed like an autumn sunset. He sat next to her and pulled out three enlarged black and white prints.

"Oh, you were so sweet and handsome." She flushed a little, realising how close to her body he was. She pretended she hadn't noticed and contemplated his perfectly sculpted face. "You haven't changed much", she teased fancifully.

"I know." His amazing eyes held her gaze firmly but gracefully. It was terrifying but so exciting and beautiful. She had never wanted a man so badly. He lit up so much fire and lust inside her fragile frame. The flames in his eyes, she could not extinguish nor the burning heat plundering her unresisting body. She just wanted to close her eyes and kiss him. If she didn't kiss him soon, she thought she would faint.

He bent over gently; the throbbing muscles in his arms clasped her body tightly. Then he gently planted a kiss on her cheek. It was hugely satisfying. A cocktail of enthralling sensations assailed her. She closed her eyes overtaken by the immensity of the moment. But the hunger engulfing her was unbearable.

"Thank you for a lovely evening, Julia. You were absolutely divine."

Julia just didn't know what to say. She returned a smile of sorts tinged with disappointment. She was sad the evening was about to come to an abrupt conclusion. She so much hoped it could go on forever. She needed the excitement ravishing her body to go on and on and on. She knew that making love to Franco would be the ultimate orgasmic ecstasy it was meant to be. She just knew, she wanted him to mount her there and then and take her where she had never been before. This was no illusion. She knew it with absolute certainty. For the first time she wasn't regretting having lost the battle of wits to a stronger man, a gentleman.

Franco looked at his watch. It was four o'clock in the morning and the sky was almost ready to welcome another day.

"I'll show you to your room. If you like, Fred can sleep next to your bed."

She got up and followed him to her room. Everything inside the guest bedroom glowed white, the duvet, the furniture, the doors, the curtains. Picasso's Guernica overhanging her enormous bed stood out like a large jig-saw of grotesque shapes in a sea of white.

"Good night." he said, musingly. So, clouds did have a silver lining after all he thought even dark sinister ones.

"Good night." she replied.

Chapter 5

Julia slept fitfully that night. She spent the early hours of the new day staring at the white ceiling, thinking about the mammoth events of the previous night. She was starting to realise her life had just changed drastically. The refreshing independence she treasured so much which had literally lit up her humdrum lifestyle was in real danger of vanishing into thin air and with it, her great plans, her career and her prized shoe store.

She looked at Fred lying in a roll on the duvet cushioning her feet. The Labrador too seemed to have slept fitfully. It constantly changed its posture seeking a more comfortable position.

"Julia." There was a gentle knock on her door. "Are you awake? Are you decent?"

She squinted at the alarm clock in shock. It was practically midday. She must have nodded off the last time she looked at the clock. It was only seven thirty then. The door handle turned and Franco's head popped in.

"Are you decent?"

The warm rapport established the previous night had vanished as though it had never happened. He was in his blue silk dressing gown, a soft blue matching his eyes. There being no reply from Julia, he calmly walked up to her, his long legs covering the distance in half the time she would, leant over her, kissed her on her forehead and sat on the edge of her bed.

"Did you sleep well?"

She nodded and smiled.

"My God, you are beautiful."

There was a firm, primeval pull in his voice, primeval and irresistible. It brought a sudden fluttering to her chest and she was scared to look at him. Her eyes focussed on his hands, clasped on his lap. Her heart contracted with something between fear and pain. The resentful passion of old resurfaced and she was starting to panic.

"Do you normally visit your guests when they're still in bed?"

"After a late night I always love to serve them breakfast in bed. I always thought it was a nice touch." There was a deliberate, mocking snare in his voice which she hated. With it came an unbearable burst of excitement which scared her out of her wits "unless you want to sleep some more."

"No, that's okay." She shook her head and gave a sharp sigh.

"Good. So what shall it be?"

As she wondered what an Italian brunch would comprise of his gaze rested on her dishevelled, honey-comb locks and he ran his fingers through them. With every moment that passed he was degrading her to the mercy of desire. She just didn't know how to deal with it. But she knew exactly what he was doing.

"What are you doing? I thought you promised," she groaned remotely.

But his mind was miles away at that moment. He was on some distant dream island, sitting beneath a palm tree, amorously running his fingers through his sweetheart's beautiful hair. For a second time his smooth, firm fingers caressed her soft silky curls. It was even more unbearable than before and she had to close her eyes to cope with the assault of sensations on her numb nerves. His hand then glided down to the nape of her neck and started to massage and gently squeeze, setting off a salvo of surges and shocks inside her. She didn't know if it was his smooth sophistication, his devious way of catching her unawares or her hormones that had gone berserk. The only thing she knew was if this went on any longer she was going to kiss him on his lips. The growing hunger inside her was devouring her entrails. She was on the verge of surrendering to a stronger power.

"So," he said as he stood up. "Will it be bacon and sausages, with tomatoes, mushrooms, fried eggs, toast and coffee or continental?"

"Just coffee and toast please." She desperately struggled to find her voice beyond the violent emotions strangling her. "But not in bed. I'm not accustomed to this sophistication. I'll take a quick shower and get dressed first. She prayed she could regain her composure quickly enough and try to control this devil of a situation much better than she had so far.

"Can I join you?" he squinted at her mockingly.

"For breakfast, maybe," she retorted.

When she walked into the brightly lit and airy kitchen, he was sitting, nibbling his toast and looking at the morning papers.

"I hope you don't mind staying in the kitchen. I always have breakfast in here. Less stuff to wash up unless you prefer to …."

"No, no, kitchen is fine," Her voice conveyed complete control and composure now. She poured herself some coffee and fresh cream, then spread a thin coat of marmalade on her toast.

"You look even more ravishing now," he teased. "So, what do you want to do today?" he asked unexpectedly.

"Do?" she heard herself ask.

"A dip in the pool perhaps first?" Amusement oozed from his eyes.

"No, I don't think so."

"A walk in the woods, picking mushrooms or truffles?" he grinned amiably.

She shook her head at the young rascal in him and an easy silence followed, soothing her nerves. For a long moment they looked at each other but neither broke the silence. He was happy to give her a bit of time and space to take in the new surroundings and the unexpected turn of events. She admired his controlled masculinity and his patience and wanted to learn from him. If only to wrench some control from him and run her own destiny the way she really wanted.

Franco put the paper down and poured himself some more hot coffee.

"So, are you going to tell me the real purpose of your visit to Milano?" His brows arched above the seductive, deep sea-blue globes contemplating her every movement. "If it's not a young Italian lover that brings you here, it's got to be shoes then. Is it shoes?" The humourless curve of his lips betrayed a trace of jealousy which his thin smile failed to veil.

Shrugging, she took a deep breath realising telling little white lies would serve no purpose. Now, because of the unexpected events of the previous twenty-four hours he would sooner or later discover the truth. He gracefully waited for her answer, his eyelashes motionless but his eager curiosity itching at his finger-tips.

"So?" His twisted lips, stark and humourless, made her increasingly self-conscious. "It can't just be a little break, can it?"

"Well, a bit of both, I suppose. I needed some quality time to myself and what better place than Milan, with its chic cultural, fashion outlets and sophistication. I knew I wouldn't get bored here. And then the shoes too."

"You've a way with words, haven't you? You put it really nicely." His tones rang like music to her ears. "So it is the shoes after all."

An odd little smile danced on his sensuous lips. "You know, if you want I can help you."

She honestly wanted to do this all by herself. That was the whole point of it. What pleasure or satisfaction would there be in it if she asked someone else to do the hard work for her? Anyway, she had already made a step by step plan in her mind. Travelling to Milan, the cradle of stylish footwear was the first of many significant steps which would finally deliver her dream. Her mission was about to take off. What pride was there for her if she was going to become a bystander? She wanted to learn the hard way, the only way that could benefit her. If she really needed a helping hand she could always ask for it.

Julia's thoughts must have mapped themselves out across her face for a sardonic smile stretched the corners of Franco's perfectly formed mouth. He said nothing.

"Well, it's very kind of you but at the moment my mind is set on doing this myself. It's a learning curve which I'm really enjoying."

She allowed herself a few cosy moments, bathing in the warm rays emanating from his gorgeous eyes. In an odd sort of way she was pleased he had offered her his services. If she ever needed them at least she would not find it so forbidding now to ask. Incredibly, the huge difference between their personalities, history and professions allowed for some affinity in the way they thought. A few hours earlier she would have found it horrifying, odious and unbearable. But now it was perfectly congenial. Not only that, but there was a virtuous catholic charisma watching over her every time their eyes met.

On the other hand she was beginning to feel there was no hiding place from him, not even in her most intimate thoughts. She was like an open book to him. There she was in Milan naively thinking she could enjoy the stress-free lifestyle of an incognito for a week while she set up her future.

"Well, the offer is there if you need it, Julia", he teased again.

"Thank you, Franco. But I'll be fine. Honestly."

Her firm retort lifted her heart and sent a breeze of satisfaction through her lungs. She had to defend her territory or soon she wouldn't be able to call her dream hers any more. This was her thing and no one was going to take away any part of it from her. After all, Franco was still only an acquaintance of sorts despite her having just slept in one of his beds. Granted he was her host and he hadn't made her pay for her room but that didn't give him the right to run her life. Reluctantly she was a guest at his villa and guests didn't relinquish their right to freedom of movement or the ownership of their thoughts.

Plainly he was a distinctly assertive man and it showed in his calm poise and in the way he moved and spoke, always with such measured aplomb. He gazed pleasurably at her, enthralled by the sexiness of her flushed face. His eyes travelled along her slim frame, from head to toes, and vice-versa, deliberately dallying on the soft contours of her breasts.

"You're a terrific girl, you know." he smiled feverishly.

"You're so beautiful and undeniably talented even if a little scared."

"I'm not scared." she said harshly, lying through her teeth and blushing a little more. "What makes you think that?"

"But I like that," he grinned, dismissing her question like an admonished school girl.

"I like you a lot. I guess you already know that." He paused scouring her face for any positive reaction.

"Don't you like me at all?"

"If I hadn't met you last night", she said dismissively," I'd be scouring all the shoe stores in the galleria by now looking for little gems for my shop."

She flinched convinced she had just committed another gaffe. She was playing into his hands at every juncture and soon she was going to be completely at his mercy and wouldn't he like that? It was high time she just shut up, got dressed and left before he had time to make his next move. She knew that each and every move in his strategy would have been carefully planned and simulated in his mind so he could execute it to perfection.

Her mind was in turmoil. Lifting her gaze she felt a shrill chill invade her body from top to bottom and she felt powerless under his hypnotic sway. His force of will and his sexual supremacy were a Goliath of an adversary and she simply was no match. He stood up and started to walk around the table. It made her more edgy but she followed his movement from the corner of her eyes.

"Julia, if you only stop thinking of me as a rival, as someone who is trying to compete with you or take something away from you", he gently tilted his head, "it would be so much better for both. As it happens, I've some important contacts here, people who can really make a difference to your exciting venture. Don't be so naïve; you're going to need all the help you need when you start a business as challenging as yours. It's still your shop for heaven's sake and you still make the decisions. Trust me on this."

His unruffled matter-of-fact tone annoyed her. She knew deep down he was probably making good sense but she still felt it would be a huge compromise and a cheap capitulation. Sure she would make a few mistakes on the way but wasn't that the whole point of it all? Therein lay the learning process, all the fun and excitement of a treasure hunt of sorts. To take all that away, would make it another lack-lustre chore bereft of heart and soul.

His circular stroll round the kitchen came to a stop behind her. He gently placed his hands on her shoulders setting off an army of shivers down her spine. He massaged her neck with growing intensity and gently lowered his masterful fingers towards her bosom.

"Don't." she groaned.

But even her voice failed her. Betrayed once again by her retreating defences and her own feelings, she felt her nipples tighten. She stiffened to try and resist the salvo of euphoric arrows raiding her senses but it was too late.

"You confound me. I can't work out what to do with you Julia. The moment I'm next to you I just can't help it. You drive me crazy. I want to make love to you all the time and when it's over I want to start all over again."

Please stop, she begged him in her mind but she couldn't think straight anymore as she too was going crazy. Desire glowed in her smoky eyes and in every sinew of her body.

"Oh God." she whispered.

He leant over her and showered the nape of her neck with wet kisses that sent her revolving into an ecstatic galaxy of amazing sensations. She couldn't take it anymore. It was an enigmatic, heavenly torment willing her to yield. She stood up, held his muscular torso close to her hardened nipples and with her hungry tongue tasted the unctuous cocktail oozing from his wet lips and his firm, craggy tongue. At that moment she would have gone anywhere with him, done anything he said, her entire being was at his mercy. The mere thought of her unconditional surrender to this towering, hypnotic deity terrified her. She thought she was losing her mind but she couldn't let go. Her intoxicated body yearned for more. The sensations plundering her every muscle pulled her to him ever so tightly.

When their mouths separated, his unquenched thirst for her was not diminished. His yearning mouth explored her smooth neck and his hands playfully caressed the contours of her breasts eventually climbing to grasp her red-hot nipples. She quivered restlessly and her legs could hardly support her a moment longer. But feeling her slipping away, he lifted her in his strong arms and gently placed her on the table, carefully trying to shove the plates to one side. Unfortunately she sat on a slice of toast that had spilled over and she started to giggle awkwardly.

Once Franco realised the source of her laughter, he too joined in and both declared a truce. A long silence ensued, somewhere between bashful satisfaction, mutual admiration and uncertainty. But it wasn't an awkward silence, more like a relaxed visual exchange without the encumbering weight of words.

When they had both showered and got dressed, Julia accepted Franco's offer to meet one of his childhood friends who ran a shoe factory just outside Milan. His name was Giancarlo. She couldn't believe what an effortless decision it was for her, despite her initial qualms clawing at her heart, her fears and initial reservations that had sent a cloud of despair over her. She crossed her fingers and prayed it would be an invaluable godsend to finally launch her dream with a champagne-popping bang.

She said very little in the car and throughout the journey kept her fingers crossed under her handbag, out of Franco's sight. She was very excited about the new prospects but frightened and a little insecure too. Giancarlo turned out quite a hot dish himself so much so Julia started to wonder whether there were any unattractive Italian men. She certainly hadn't seen any in Milan.

"Are all men so handsome here?" Julia whispered into Franco's ear.

Franco flinched, raised his eyebrows and shrugged his shoulders. Then he compressed his lips. "Shall we ask Giancarlo?" he whispered back.

"No, no." She flushed to her hairline. "It was just a thought."

"Ask me what?" Giancarlo grinned, frowning at Franco.

"Oh, it's nothing." The embarrassment ran all over her cheeks.

"Julia thinks you're handsome, Gianni."

"Franco?"

Julia couldn't believe he had the cheek to embarrass her so. How could he? This was obviously not a good idea at all. Accepting his offer had been another misjudgement. Why she even started to trust him in the first place was completely beyond her comprehension.

"Oh, thank you. I'm afraid, there's a beautiful wife and three gorgeous angels at home."

"Franco was just being silly," protested Julia as she braced herself for this extraordinary treat. She wasn't going to allow a little impish tease ruin the visit. Even though she was a little annoyed, she thought she'd rather have a playful, rascal edge to a man than condescending insolence. But the two coming together in the same man was a paradox she couldn't start to explain to herself.

"So, I'll run you through the factory first." His voice was full of freshness and enthusiasm.

"As you can see, we do have machinery but most of the intricate work on every shoe is done by hand. It's a labour of love that goes into making our shoes and every worker in my factory has been personally trained and vetted by my father Giuliano. Before they're even allowed in here they must make twelve faultless pairs and they must wear them to appreciate the comfort of a good pair of shoes. Then they can start."

"A very impressive strategy," Julia was intoxicated by the heavy scent of raw leather which hugged her nostrils. It was like being in one of those wine-tasting sanctuaries in the Loire Valley or in the Aquitaine region of France.

"Isn't it quite?" Franco said harshly, briefly winking at her.

"I told you you'd be in your element here. Shall we move to the sales quarters now and look at the finished product?" He led the way as he spoke.

Giancarlo indicated the way forward and politely ushered Julia ahead of him. In the showroom Julia was overwhelmed by the rich variety, the exotic display of colour and shapes and that refined, dreamy scent of the finished masterpieces. It was like an exclusive museum housing the royalty of footwear and she was the special guest for the day.

"So, *Signorina* Julia, can you see anything you like?" teased Giancarlo.

"I think the question should be is there anything I don't like?" she said, her eyes afire. "And the answer is no. Nothing. I love everything."

"Good, good," arbitrated Franco in his distinctive harsh tones ringing across the large hall.

Julia had the time of her life picking a choicest selection among those eye-pleasing jewels, each one a winner in its own right. She had already worked out in her mind exactly where she'd place them in her own store. With so much glamour, originality and class in her shop she would soon be the toast of the South of England let alone Bournemouth. A taste of Milan in sunny Bournemouth. Who could argue with that?

Giancarlo was a true gentleman in his exquisite, chivalrous manners, in his honest business acumen and his extravagant generosity. He gave Julia the most favourable prices and credit terms she could have ever expected. She was so incredulous of her good fortune she almost cried when she signed the papers.

"I couldn't resist making you such good offers." confessed Giancarlo later that afternoon as they lunched at a nearby *'albergo'*. "When you're starting a new business, you need all the help you can get."

"And more." said Franco.

"*Signorina* Julia, it's been indeed a great pleasure doing business with you today and I hope it's the start of a long and successful partnership."

"Thank you." smiled Julia, regally. "I'm awfully grateful for all your help and for an amazing day. I've thoroughly enjoyed myself. And I certainly hope what we started to day will continue for a very long time to our mutual satisfaction. And success, of course."

"It couldn't happen to a nicer girl," Franco chipped in, teasingly." His sweet words caressed her nerves.

"I'm glad you took up my offer, Julia."

"So am I, "she gracefully replied.

"Good, "said Franco, making sure he had the last word on the matter.

"I hope you're equipped with a little warehouse back home."

"I do have a garage, Franco, which should be large enough."

Later that evening they sat by the pool sipping a celebratory Champagne followed by a mix of Single Malts right into the small hours. It was a balmy evening with a strong scent of pine in the air.

Julia hadn't had the time to take in the true magnitude of the events that had just taken over her life and they were enormous, that much she knew. Only days earlier, there had been moments when she wondered what on earth she was doing embarking on such a grandiose and crazy venture. As for the probability of her pulling the whole thing off, she had only given herself two out of a possible ten. Even with Lindsey helping her. Now she knew her chances of success were sky high but she wouldn't want to tempt fate with a premature rush of optimism. Restraint was of the essence.

"By the way, Franco," she remembered. "When I whisper something into your ears it's for your ears only. I'd have thought that was self-evident." She looked at him ruefully.

Franco lifted his dark brows but didn't utter a word. Julia found his unflappable conceit frustrating. In some ways it was much easier to deal with a courteous, refined man like Giancarlo. But having to constantly wrestle with Franco's ruthlessly raw clout was jangling her nerves. He was a relentless menace and she needed to consider very carefully every word she said and every possible consequence that might ensue. She took a long sip from her misty crystal glass to lubricate her dry throat.

"Why did you try to embarrass me this afternoon in front of Giancarlo? There was absolutely no need for that." She frowned and sipped a little more.

His grin was full of amusement. "Giancarlo is a good mate, Julia. It was only a little tease. He can take it, he's a grown man."

"Of course he can take it. The joke was on me. That's why." She was almost livid now. She could scoff or shout at him but nothing seemed to unnerve his supreme poise and confidence.

"Alright, point taken. I take full blame for my sin." He gazed at her lovingly. "It was very tactless of me and I hold my hands up."

"Tactless? It was damn rude, childish and if it was meant to be a joke, then it was definitely not funny and in bad taste." Her gaze sank, as did her words, into the still waters of the pool.

"Julia, you have to understand where I come from, nothing is sacred. We make jokes about anything sometimes a little irreverently too. Not even churches or funerals are exempt. When I was a young boy, we used to do anything for a cheap laugh. We even switched gravestones once. And I remember as an altar boy I hid the priest's glasses at Sunday Mass. It was hilarious, so much laughter among the parishioners."

"Oh, should that make me feel any better now?" A sudden chill tensed her skin.

"I did say I was sorry." The words reached her ears hard and without a grain of emotion. "Anyway", he went on, "I got you something I think you'll like."

Julia flashed him a look of surprise. But before she could even express her indifference with some witty remark, he had got up and fetched a pink shopping bag. Then he gleefully fished out a slick, two piece swim suit which he placed on front of her.

"Put it on and let's take a dip."

Without thought Julia picked it up and regaled her eyes. But before her impulsiveness ran away with her, she put it down again.

"Thanks but I don't think so."

Instantly, she noticed his jaws tighten and the disappointment in his eyes sent an electric current fizzing up her limbs and straight to her spine.

"Oh, you've to put in on now, Julia, I got it for you." It was a firm forbidding voice, more like a command than a polite invitation.

"I want to see you wear it and swim in it. The water is warm, don't worry."

She had either gone crazy or had completely lost the plot. Or maybe the alcohol she had just consumed was doing the thinking for her. She slipped out of her dress and her underwear and gingerly put on the minuscule suit without even a thought. Franco helped her fasten the bra and then suddenly changed his mind. He unfastened it again and flung it mischievously into the pool.

"Swim topless." It was an action that left her little choice. He grinned and gently ran his finger down the small of her back. She quivered with excitement. The desire in his eyes grew. He held her head in his hands and nuzzled the nape of her slim neck lingeringly. Neither spoke but the closeness of their bodies satisfied a fierce hunger inside them. Her throat dried up and her body froze, yearning with more hunger. She realised then how starved she had been of his uncompromising touch. He ran his lips teasingly along her neck with a swelling intensity, flooding her in a pool of dark sensuality the like of which she had never known. He then cupped his hand under her chin, turned her head until his predator's mouth met hers and supremely explored her vulnerability.

Then as they were both enraptured in a whirlwind of lust, desire and ecstasy her feet gave way, plunging them both into the pool, she in her topless swimsuit, Franco still wearing his checked Lambretta shirt, pressed trousers and snake-skin shoes. It was an unexpected cold shower initially for both in spite of the heated water. Franco laughed, flung his shoes back on to dry land and grappled with his belt trying to slip out of his trousers. Then his shirt came off. Meanwhile Julia coughed relentlessly having swallowed what seemed like a gallon of chlorine. Her throat was sore, her eyes ached and her ears jangled.

She soon recovered though as Franco swam up to her and kissed her. Still wielding his belt, he ran it featherlike down the small of her back unleashing a rampant furore inside her. Her blood started to surge again spawning pockets of excitement. He then pulled her body close to his, floated on his back and carried her to the shallow end. Lifting her in his arms he couldn't help exploring her taut crimson nipples and her luscious breasts sprinkled with shimmering droplets.

She was a feast of curves, silky paleness and dreamy scents. Something incomprehensible in her head willed her hands toward him running it over his tight skin of his chest. Every muscle in her body surrendered to the rhythm of his heaving heartbeat. The caution in her head was no match to the enormity of her desire. The palm of her hand slid sensuously over his dark, abrasive chest, then her hungry mouth followed suit, lingeringly exploring every inch of his taut skin, eventually rising to satisfy her hunger for his strong neck. Ablaze with fire and exultation she gasped. She couldn't believe her frail body could contain such a crushing cocktail of volcanic sensations. But she didn't want it to stop. Her rapturous eyes pleaded for more.

"If you only knew how long I've waited for this moment." his voice was deep and brutal.

The honesty of the moment was overwhelming. She closed her eyes and savoured his dark skin. A sudden explosion of fluid inside her shook her very entrails, her thighs quivered and she desperately bit her lip so hard that blood almost flowed.

"I want you so much." he croaked as he savagely crushed her breasts under his tight grip.

The pain in his face intrigued her but her own pain excited her. Sharp jagged stabs plundered her wilfully but her aching breasts craved for more. She willed him to pull her nipples, to suck them and bite them and drive her insane till she was completely lost in a wondrous spell of ecstatic opulence.

"Me too." she groaned. "Please don't stop." It was hardly a whisper. "I want you …..I want you inside me."

Her words tailed off into the silent darkness and Franco was too engrossed in his own primeval needs to hear. She shuddered, embarrassed and a little alarmed at her own words. As if Franco needed any encouragement. A moment of frustration squirmed through her. But she hardly had time to gasp when he heaved at her breasts once again. Her mouth trembled and she sighed wanting to touch herself too. He finally closed in on her nipple and sucked and pulled and plundered. She cried out. For a long moment his weight pushed her under the water and she thought she was going to choke. But she still yearned for more. His head too sank under the surface as his mouth caressed her thighs, titillating her sensations.

As they resurfaced for breath, she thrust her hips close to his, hugged him tightly and pierced her fingers into his back, leaving little red fingerprints. Her confidence soared as never before.

"You're good at this, aren't you?" He suddenly teased.

The corners of her mouth curved but she was intoxicated with too much frustrating passion to be able to smile. Her sexuality was still throbbing under his influence. He lifted her in his arms, kissed her mouth and her breasts and stepped out of the pool.

"I'm hungry now," He said firmly. "And you?"

She shuddered feeling the cooler air brushing against her damp, pale skin and nodded obediently. Her dazed eyes could not hide the growing disappointment in them despite the sea of shimmering green. She looked at her aching breasts, compressed her lips as if in an apologetic gesture and started to dry herself.

"Just something light, please." Her voice was husky. She wasn't really hungry. She was exhausted and breathed with difficulty. She just wanted to shower and go to bed to catch up on her sleep.

Later on that night as they sat in the kitchen nibbling away at their steak sandwich they spent long periods staring at each other. They were both quite tired. So much had changed in such a short time it was an unwieldy undertaking thinking about it, let alone discussing it. Where would they start?

"I hope you enjoyed yourself today," he said harshly.

"Very much," she retorted.

"Good. I'm glad." He pulled her to him and gently kissed her mouth, licking off a spot of ketchup.

"Nice." He smiled. "So why are you looking so glum suddenly?"

"Oh," she said almost tormented and almost apologetically. "You know, I think I'd better fly back home tomorrow."

His brows lifted and his eyes popped out in shock.

"What? You can't do that Julia." His voice was barbaric. "Are you crazy? You've just signed the best deal of your life with one of the top shoe producers in Europe. Don't you know what that means? You've joined an elite dynasty now. You don't realise, do you, how your life has changed in a matter of hours, and I'm not referring to you and me here.

"I know," she agreed.

"I've got a top brand on board which is great. But I'm not suddenly going to adopt a lavish lifestyle and start to squander money I haven't even earned yet. And I've still got to pay for them."

"That is true, Julia. Having stock is money well spent. But I'm talking about a balanced lifestyle. All work and no play, is bad for business. In no time you'll wear yourself out. Your business needs you at your best at all times. That's where leisure and relaxation come in. Recharging batteries must be built into your lifestyle. That's what successful professionals do."

"But Franco, I haven't got a business yet."

"Julia, you've just signed an important contract with a new business partner who also becomes a friend in social circles, especially here in Italy. We keep everything in perspective and you do better business if the people you work with are friends too. And an added bonus for you, here, the men always pay. You provide the exquisite company, the grace and the beauty. We are only too happy to pay for that sterling service."

"Franco, I'm not some uneducated blond from some old-school period drama, you know. When I go out I don't go out to service anyone. I go out on my own terms and I pay my way. That's the way it's always been and always will be."

"Oh, I know we disagree vehemently on this topic so I'm not even going to argue. The point is, tomorrow …. Are you listening?" he tapped the air as he spoke. "Well, tomorrow we are invited for the day on Giancarlo's Cabin Cruiser. He keeps it on the Lago di Garda. And the weather forecast for the day is excellent. So, how about that?"

The horror on Julia's face would have chilled anyone. Not Franco, though. He contemplated her, unmoved, sitting still, stiff as the Mona Lisa, her mouth open but unable to utter a single sound.

"And more," he went on, his mouth stretching into an uncompromising grin. "Are you ready for this? The day after tomorrow, I've got you a date with another big shoe producer, just outside Verona. So Lady, brace yourself for two very eventful days ahead of you. And don't get faint-hearted now. This can be the start of something very, very special."

"Franco, thank you but ….." She was lost for words and didn't know what to feel. Should she scream in frustration or jump for joy? "I don't think I'm ready for this. I haven't even had time to take it in, nothing has sunk in yet, Franco. Please I need time and space to think and work things out for myself. This is much too hasty for me."

"Julia," His harsh tone was admonishing her weakening resolve. "You can have as much time and space as you need. It's not a problem. It's normal. But don't go throwing it all away now. You've taken an amazing step and I'm not trying to undermine what you've accomplished so far."

She shook her head and took a deep breath. "I really don't know about this. Please don't take it wrongly. It's not that I am not grateful for everything you've done. Of course I am." She was afraid of sounding disingenuous and shallow. "I will be indebted for ever to you."

He threw his arms around her and kissed her, once more shattering her defences. She swallowed and stiffened desperate to stay in control. She kept telling herself maybe it is time she should trust him a little bit more. But doubts about her ability to cope and stay in charge surfaced and swarmed around her.

"Trust me, Julia." He squeezed her body even closer. "Please, have I let you down so far?"

She shook her head meekly.

"No, you've been an absolute gentleman. And I've loved every moment. And that's the honest truth."

"You don't really know how beautiful you are. You do something to me which no other girl does. And you have shown me you do like me too, hopefully as much as I like you." He paused, his eyes resting on hers, oozing with tormented passion. "I wanted to make love to you so much tonight," kissing her gently on her mouth. "But I didn't want to rush things this time. I didn't want you to think it was another one night thing. I don't want you to run away. I'm not just after a night of lust and sexual gratification. It's you I want, beautiful body, beautiful soul and above all your beautiful mind I want to get into and share with you. There."

Her emerald eyes filled up, her stomach fluttered and chills rang down her spine. She hugged him tightly and once more surrendered her mouth to his overpowering sway.

Chapter 6

The next morning after a token breakfast, they met Giancarlo outside his own villa, transferred their bags stuffed with supplies into his silver Mercedes waiting on his drive and within minutes they were tearing up the Autostrada on their way to Como.

Sitting by herself on the back seat Julia elusively re-ran the momentous events of the previous day. But regrets soon rankled inside her and doubts about the wisdom of her presence in the car too. Why was she deserting her valued resolutions, her principles and the confidence in pursuing her dream independently? She had naively allowed Franco to tug her along on a dangerously different journey and she had no idea where it would take her.

She obviously hadn't learnt one single lesson from experience and her resolve had been wanting once again. When was she going to learn Business and Pleasure just couldn't mix without one getting in the way of the other? She couldn't allow her primal yearning for passion and sexual gratification to subjugate her will, her ambition, her whole being. But how was she going to restrain herself, stay in control if every time Franco touched her or even looked at her a superior driving force brushed her pathetic defences ruthlessly aside and assumed complete control?

The anguish burning in her eyes must have grabbed Giancarlo's attention in his rear-view mirror.

"*Tutto va bene Julia?*"

"Yes, I'm fine. I was miles away, thinking." A hint of pink and a polite smile faintly veiled her apprehension.

"It's not my driving is it that's worrying you?"

"No, no. it's fine, honestly." She lifted her chin and desperately tried to buoy up the tone of her voice.

"You're very quiet," Franco chipped in. "What are you thinking of?"

"Everything and nothing, you know. A woman's prerogative, a little day-dreaming."

"No, no. Not quite." Giancarlo relaxed his foot on the accelerator.

Julia gave a sigh of approval. It's not that she didn't trust Giancarlo's driving. He seemed a very competent and safe driver. But since the infamous, tragic death of Princess Diana she had developed an aversion to sitting in the back of posh Mercedes cars, particularly on fast motorways. Or whatever they called them in Italy.

"You can relax, Julia." said Franco in a neutral, quasi-robotic monotone. "I can assure you, you won't find a safer driver than Gianni. I trust him with my life."

Giancarlo acknowledged the compliment with a suitable smile and Franco underlined his confession with a string of little nods.

"I do believe you. But sitting in the back makes you feel a bit more vulnerable."

"Hey, you could fall asleep in the back and go to Wonderland and back. This car is so smooth nothing would disturb your sleep."

Giancarlo's reassuring voice did little to dispel her apprehension. If anything, she was starting to dread the day ahead of her.

Franco turned, revealing his incisive profile. "You're not tired, are you?"

"Oh, no." she lied through her teeth. His chiselled contour gave her goose-bumps.

"I'll be fine."

She wished Lindsey could be by her side and she suddenly remembered she hadn't even replied to her text from the previous night. What would she think of her? She might even worry something might have happened to her. She was tempted to text her there and then but she knew perfectly well she would return her call instantly. She couldn't really talk to her properly with the two men eavesdropping. Lindsey was not naïve. She would soon suspect something was amiss even though everything was really fine. That's the way God made Lindsey.

    Finally, she made her mind up and sent her a brief text reassuring her everything was fine and that she would call her back soon when she had a moment to herself. She then quickly switched off her mobile, replaced it inside her beige leather handbag and closed her eyes for a few moments.

"Don't fall asleep now, Julia." Franco said crisply, turning round to check on her. "We're almost there."

She flinched at the sudden intrusion of his voice into her moment of equanimity.

"That's great." she huskily replied. Her heart sank in dismay but she immediately banished every thought of fear and apprehension, promising herself she was going to enjoy every minute. After all, when would she get another chance to spend a day like this, cruising on the most famous lake in Italy on a millionaire's private boat, escorted by two outrageously handsome hunks? Not in a million years.

A few minutes later there she was, basking snugly in bright sunshine, in her Italian sunshades on the deck of the *'Ramazzotti'*. Giancarlo had called his boat after a famous Italian singer who was his childhood idol. Both men had changed into their starched, snow-white shorts and white polo shirts just like the two men crew. But she didn't really have anything suitable to wear; this had come as a huge surprise to her not giving her time to go anywhere.

As they set off cutting into the still blue waters of the Garda, Franco approached her, holding a white wafer-like box and an ironic smile lurking on his lips. She froze hoping against hope it wasn't another skimpy bathing suit. There was no way she was going to wear it, not in front of strangers. She had acquiesced to most of his wishes so far but there was a limit to her gracious affability. She shook her head before he had even opened his mouth.

"Franco please, not here, I'm not going to make a show of myself." she said clenching her fist for strength.

"Open it first, Julia." They were harsh tones that demanded instant respect.

"No, I'd rather not." she said shortly.

"It's not what you think it is. Honestly open it." His voice was softer but his eyes stabbed incisively as he held out the box to her. She stood her ground still refusing to take the box from him. He gave her a look he would give to an untamed stallion, unblinking and equal to the challenge. "Julia," he went on, pursing his pink lips, "It's a gift from Giancarlo. He asked me to give it to you myself as a gesture for accepting his invitation."

"I see," She uttered feeling suddenly stupid.

"It's only polite to open it and accept it." It was a level tone but equally lethal in intention.

"I'm sorry." Her chin lifted and she grabbed the box from him. Then she walked up to Giancarlo, kissed him gently on his cheek and proceeded to open the surprise gift, source of all the angst so far.

"It's beautiful. Thank you Giancarlo." She kissed him again. "I'm truly flattered."

"Won't you put them on?"

It was a matching two piece leisure suit by Versace comprising a lemon V-shaped top with matching shorts. These had a thin, white contour in silk, a smart coup de grace in any couturier's book. She couldn't wait to put them on.

When she emerged from the cabin Franco's face lit up like a flame.

"You look fabulous."

"Thank you," she said, her voice saturated with something between joy and embarrassment. Franco kissed her lingeringly on her lips and held her in his arms till his lips yielded.

"I love them." she said with a glance at her slick shorts. She couldn't stop her eyes from wandering across to his abrasive, muscular legs. She was itching to run the palm of her hand down the back of his legs but she couldn't find the courage to do so, not in the presence of another men. It would send a whirlwind of sensations through her body. All the erotic dreams she had about him would return to haunt her. Franco had well and truly bewitched her in spite of her half-hearted resistance and she hoped the entrapment was mutual. But now wasn't the moment.

At regular intervals the cruiser eased up and they drew her attention to historic landmarks. There were castles, palatial mansions looming above their own extensive parks, minuscule medieval towers nestled on cliff edges and a stunning coastline laced with sprawling pines and firs and acacias that were an enchantment to behold. On one bank a cluster of quaint pavilions, probably constructed by some rich Marquis over the turn of the century as a summer retreat, broke the line of gleaming green. To Julia it was like visiting the most thrilling open-air art museum on the planet. She was so glad she had been invited. It would have been utter madness to decline such an enthralling offer. Pure delight excited her as she took it all in. The warm sunshine on her skin doubled her pleasure. She was sure the boat trip would remain in the forefront of her memory for months to come.

A bunch of grey clouds approached on the hazy horizon, occasionally allowing the sunrays to flicker through them, setting off a playful display of flares and flashes on the surface of the water. Franco joined the pilot and took over the steering, a charge obviously familiar to him as he executed it with the utmost precision and mastery. Meanwhile, Giancarlo prepared lunch with Silvio, one of the crew. It wasn't long before Giancarlo returned brandishing two glasses of perfectly chilled Champagne and an array of delicious sandwiches, drumsticks, and blinis generously topped with caviar and a twist of lemon, square-shaped macaroni cakes and a variety of pizza triangles. It was the perfect feast in the most idyllic of surroundings.

"This is some treat," thought Julia casting a glance over the mouth-watering, colourful spread.

"Oh just a little snack," he sat next to her and offered her the bubbly. "You need to be able to enjoy the view before you build an appetite."

"Thank you. I think you're right. I've to admit I do feel peckish now." She looked into his dark hazel gaze and she sensed why he was so successful. His noble manners twinned with his gentle ways belied a hard ambitious man armed with a steely determination.

"Do you do this often then?"

"Not as often as I would like, unfortunately. But I do bring the family out here when I can. The kids love it. They love to fish from the boat. They're in boarding school at the moment and my wife is too busy travelling around the country."

"Oh really," Julia was bowled over.

"You sound a little surprised?" The edges of his cute mouth curled in bemusement. "You see, she is a journalist for *'La Reppublica'* and travel is an essential part of her job. Besides, she loves travelling especially on her own without having to drag me around. It works very well for both of us." His slim chin lifted. "And you?"

Julia cringed as if under a cold shower.

"What do you mean?" She didn't even know why she asked that. It was perfectly obvious what he meant. "Oh, you mean am I happy?"

He smiled. He knew very well it wasn't a trick question. "I noticed you're not wearing a ring."

"Oh, I'm single. And happy, may I add. That's why I'm embarking on this venture now, while I have time on my hands. Once you have kids it gets more difficult but I guess you know that already."

It was a tactless remark having just heard his kids were tucked away in boarding school. She hoped her comment hadn't aroused a sense of guilt in him.

"You're right. And when both parents work as in our case, it's even more difficult. But we love them to bits and when they're with us, during their school holidays, we give them all the time we can. Sometimes they get sick of us and want to do their own thing."

"I hope you didn't think I was being critical." A cool breeze thankfully brushed against her hot blushes.

"Not at all" he retorted. No offence taken." He took a long sip and smiled. "When they're at home, they rule the roost, especially the youngest. We have no say in the matter." They laughed. He stood up, walked over to the culinary delights laid out so lovingly and invited her to start indulging.

Hardly had they sat down again when Franco's voice rips through the air like a tornado.
"Gianni, E' caduto nell' aqua!"

"Chi?" retorted Giancarlo.
"Il ragazzo nella piccola barca."

There were two young boys fishing in a little boat close by and apparently one of them had suddenly disappeared under water. They swiftly manoeuvred the cruiser as close as possible to the incident. Franco tore his shirt off his brawny torso and with the celerity of a seasoned Olympian, dived into the water and swam to the little boat. He too disappeared under the water but instantly resurfaced holding a young body in his muscle-laden arm. The blond boy's frozen, statuesque attitudes had him bereft of any sign of life. His face was pale and his eyes shut. He was soon hoisted on to the deck. Franco immediately knelt next to his rock solid body, held his nose between his fingers and started to blow relentlessly into his mouth.

The dramatic event unfolding in front of Julia's very eyes entranced her in a cold sway. It was a flood of mixed emotions going through her, of admiration, amazement, fear, of reluctance to watch, but above all of complete bewitchment. The world would certainly not be the same place, she thought, without the selfless courage, bravery and adeptness of larger than life heroes. To have witnessed a dramatic rescue in real life was something else but to have witnessed Franco himself perform the act of heroism was beyond words.

In Julia's book Franco would certainly shine amongst a rare breed of men. Which girl would not admire a man who could change the course of destiny? Which girl would not go wobbly in the legs at the sight of those brawny, muscular arms, those fearless, azure eyes? But what really moved her spirit to the point of tears was his caring tenderness not witnessed till then. It was like watching King Kong, tenderly holding Jane in the palm of his hand. An intense flame rose from the pit of her stomach and a need to be held in his arms to run her lips over his abrasive, dark chest. Be kissed by those sensuous, strong lips. She sighed.

Meanwhile Giancarlo called the emergency services and a rescue helicopter was on its way. It seemed like an eternity before the boy's face stirred and his eyes opened. The dark cloud overhanging the boat suddenly lifted and the numbed muscles clamping Julia's heart released their grasp and it started to beat again. Her eyes had welled up and a solitary tear rolled down a silvery path on her cheek.

The boy finally coughed up an endless stream of water and cried. From his selfless dive into the water without even a thought for his own safety, plucking the boy heroically from the jaws of death and giving him a breathing life into his frozen limbs again, was an incredulous feat she never thought she would witness. This real larger-than-life hero had walked into her life permanently it seems. It couldn't have been more than fifteen minutes before the two youngsters were winched on to the helicopter. Everyone breathed a huge sigh of relief as they watched it soar into the distant mist. The little boat was towed away by the coast guards who had joined in the operation.

Driven by a magnetic thrill, Julia scampered up to Franco and hugged him, embracing that awesome aura oozing from his muscular frame. She couldn't think of many men who would carry out what he had just done. It was at that moment when she was starting to fall well and truly in love with him. It scared her. She shivered in his strong arms.

"How could their parents allow those toddlers alone at the mercy of the elements?" Franco asked curtly. "Don't they know how storms brew up over here without the slightest warning?" The last few droplets shimmered on his firm jaw.

Without thought Julia wiped them off with her finger.

"They probably don't even know", she said tentatively. He flashed a bemused look and planted a gentle kiss on her lips.

"You were amazing," she said unevenly.

"Just think. If we hadn't seen him, he'd be gone by now. Drowned, gone at that tender age."

"But thanks to your quick thinking, Franco, he'll be back with his grateful parents tonight." retorted Giancarlo.

"Grateful?" His voice was harsh and his face contorted into an indifferent grimace.

"Kids will always be kids." Giancarlo's

sobering voice did little to appease the irritation in Franco's eyes.

"We were the same, Franco. The lure of adventure and danger is as old as Noah's Ark. And it will never change."

"I guess not," Franco snapped, coldly.

As the crew got the cruiser on the move again, Franco's fingers tightened on Julia's and he led her to the other side of the deck where the colourful buffet had been waiting.

"This was meant to be a relaxing day," he smiled at her with a tame, almost cold tenderness in his eyes. "It wasn't meant to be so full of drama."

She cast a cautious glance at his hawkish profile, a source of fear and awe in any female's heart. But not this time and not this female, it was a more serene feeling, a guarantee of safety being in his company. The sense of well-being sent her confidence soaring. "You were just incredible, Franco. I'm so very proud and honoured to have been here with you. I shall never forget those amazing moments." Her smile soon chilled though as his cold unflappable eyes met hers.

"What can I say?" His tone was cool and earthy. "Sometimes, you get more than you bargain for." He spoke as if it had all been a regular, everyday occurrence, something he had grown perfectly accustomed to.

"You've never done this before, have you?" Caution lingered in her eyes.

"Not as dramatic as this one." His words were incisive. "On a school trip once, I had to dive and pull out a classmate from the bottom of a pool. He had jumped in rather recklessly and accidentally knocked himself out."

"Oh. How unlucky can you be?" The words leapt out of her mouth. She flushed a little. "I bet your friends looked up to you after that."

"My friends always respected me." A mischievous smile curled the edges of his mouth, "before and after. I always picked my friends carefully." He pulled her into his arms in a warm embrace. She leaned against him and hugged him tightly too.

Later that evening they continued where they had left off. She sat on his lap next to the pool in the dim sunlight. A warm breeze caressed their tanned skin. They sipped Champagne and got their teeth into some nibbles. As usual caviar was on the menu with a small spread of leftovers from the earlier buffet.

That was the best day of my life Julia was on the verge of confessing. But a dark apprehension resurfaced. Even after the amazing events of the day and although she was ready to trust him with her life there was something inside her that still held her back and it wasn't fear or anxiety. Something else, something deeper in her soul and less definable, it was something she couldn't quite put her fingers on.

He tugged her closer and kissed her. Instantly she felt the wall of his chest rise against her. Colour washed through her face and a huge appetite for his touch enveloped her like a predator's uncompromising grasp. The desperate need for him grew with every passing second. She wanted so much to take control and make sweet, brutal love to him there and then, losing herself in a gargantuan galaxy of shuddering sensations.

His mouth twisted with desire which she took as an invitation to take the lead. But her confidence suddenly faltered. She trembled with frustration and an unrequited passion. The heat scorching her thighs was unbearable.

"I want you, Julia. I want you now," his voice was firm and harsh. "I've always wanted you."

"Me too," she didn't know how many times she had dreamt of him, dreamt of this exquisite moment she thought would never happen. In her dreams she had made love to him a reckless number of times but it had never been so overpowering, so completely ecstatic and devastating. She had never thought such intense excitement could whip up so much pain and pleasure, masterfully stirred into one supreme moment.

Crying out with need and a delight the like of which she had rarely tasted, she surrendered to his glittering gaze. Lying vulnerable in his arms, yearning for the full force of his masculinity to crush her and ravish her and take her to that supreme place she had only dreamed of. Her glossy hazel eyes begged him.

He gripped her jaw firmly and turned her head. Then his taut fingers expertly protruded into her expectant mouth, sending fizzing bubbles through her tongue and every muscle in her mouth. Her blood surged through her tight veins with wondrous intensity as she fiercely tasted his salty skin.

Don't stop now, she pleaded in her heart. It was beating with the inexorable ferocity of a demented drummer. With her own itching fingers she sought his firm jaw and his hard mouth. As he withdrew his fingers, he watched with his stark honest gaze as she gently explored the expanse of his chest with her hungry tongue. She bit and pulled at his small hard nipples, exhilarated by her own daring. Never had she ever expected to be doing this to a giant of a man who had seemed so conceited, chauvinistic and impertinent, your standard one-night-stand archetype.

"Don't stop." He spoke in a soft tone. He found her fascinating as she steadily aroused his desire. She explored every exquisite inch of his vast chest, his stiff nipples and the soft contours of his belly-button. His husky voice urged her on remorselessly and his hand grabbed her hair tightly as he breathed deeply. He closed his eyes struggling hard to contain the honesty of the moment. But he was determined not to sap under the overwhelming strike of excitement. He was equal to the fierce rippling of blood and heat in his muscles.

Her lashes flickered up revealing a sea of ecstasy within. But the moment her eyes encountered the supreme charm in his, her daring deserted her. She was once again at his mercy, like a lamb for the slaughter. Her vulnerability resurfaced in awe at the firmness of his lips. Her mouth needed little or no persuasion to open up to the magic of another sensual assault. She felt fragile as her lips yielded to the blistering enthralment and her eager tongue wrestled against his. But he was now in complete control, commander-in-chief of an imminent offensive.

Before she had time to react to the frenzy of delight bubbling through her blood, his lips sucked the back of her neck, working their way around to the hub of her throat. Almost simultaneously, his hands thrust up her breasts, playfully teasing her nipples. There was no way to describe what she was feeling. These were no ordinary feelings of joy or satisfaction or sexual gratification. The volcanic sensations plundering through her were from a different constellation. It was as if her body was no more, as if it had metamorphosed into a metaphysical deity. Oh how she wished she could soar for ever on that astrophysical bubble of consummate pleasure.

"Franco." she croaked unable to open her eyes. There was little else she could say. Her blood raced, her nerves trembled and her entire body floated in space.

Jubilant at his conquest so far, Franco continued triumphantly to plunder the booty at his mercy. He squeezed her left breast in his firm grip and proceeded to suck it at the nipple, pulling and biting into it. Julia cried out in glorious pain crushing her and craving for more punishment.

"You're beautiful." His voice was harsh and brutal now. I want to ravage you till you can't scream anymore."

In complete contrast to the brutality of his tone, he lifted her in his giant arms and gently placed her on the airbed beside the pool, cushioning her head with the palm of his hand. He then lined up his formidable frame over her and prepared for the final assault.

"Tell me you want me," his soft tones were celestial music to her ears. But she was so heavily intoxicated on his terrifying sexual sway she could hardly utter a word. Her throat was parched.

"Tell me you want me, Julia," he repeated with that unmistakeable voice of audacity.

The sheer weight of his body on top of her ensured every muscle in her surrendered unconditionally to his supremacy. He slipped his hand around her neck and brutally clasped her lips between his. The blistering pain sent sharp stabs surging through her stomach. She had stopped breathing. Then the frightening desire flooding his eyes focussed on her throbbing breasts. He heaved and sucked and pulled and squeezed and even bit her nipples till she croaked in agonising ecstasy. It was a formidable paradox of unequalled delight. If there was a heaven then this had to be it. She had opened every gate allowing his soul free entry. She was ready to receive her ultimate reward, that ultimate, orgasmic summit she had craved for her entire existence.

Ablaze with consummate passion he thrust her breasts upwards and lunged at her, overflowing with the confidence of the quintessential lover. Flames of passion blazed through her as they soared with immense delight to the place of no return.

Minutes later, as they lay next to each other, staring into each other's eyes, still panting from the rapturous euphoria, Julia smiled with a joy inside her she had never felt before. At that moment she was so complete she was afraid to get up in case the moment would depart for ever.

"Thank you," she whispered.

He kissed her and threw his arms around her. They lay there for a long time in silence. "That was something else" he croaked.

Julia was still under the influence of the immense delight that had commandeered her body for most of the evening and well into the night. Now, she felt safe in his protective arms.

She knew she could trust him. She felt she could confide in him, even her most private secrets not even Lindsey knew existed. She could share stories of previous boyfriends, their fads and fetishes, their sexual prowess or shortcomings. Every subject under the sun was now an authorised subject of conversation with Franco. He had so boldly cut through her defences and expertly negotiated her surrender that she practically was his. He had finally completely won her over.

The following morning they sat in the kitchen quietly surveying their breakfast. They placidly sipped a mug of coffee and indulged in a plate of fresh strawberries and hot croissants.

"You look amazing, Julia," he said, kissing her gently on her lips.

"Thank you," She glowed at the sweet compliment.

"So," The smile in his eyes grew. "I've another little date for you today."

"Oh," She flinched, a little startled.

"We're meeting Rodolfo in Torino. He's a very successful supplier and you'll like his unique style." The glow on his face radiated over hers too. "I think you'll like him too. He's quite a hunk." He looked at his watch and picked his mug up again.

She flushed at his last remark.

"I don't know about that." Her mouth blossomed into a mischievous smile. "But I'll tell you if I do." A long easy stillness ensued punctuated only by the occasional clink of the mugs.

Suddenly, Julia's eyes clouded over. She gently bit her lower lip as she contemplated his angular jaws.

"Franco, when will you be returning to England?" she asked tentatively. She wasn't sure why she was even asking. Deep down, she'd rather he stayed in Italy. She could always open in Milan, Verona or some other amazing city in northern Italy. With him at her side and the added bonus of his reassuring expertise there could hardly be an obstacle they wouldn't be able to overcome.

He compressed his lips and shook his head.

"I don't really know, Julia. We want to launch a chain of restaurants here in the north, in Milano, Verona possibly Torino. I'm looking for prime sites and for competent people to run the different franchises."

She was shocked. "But that could take ages?"

"Well, I wouldn't say ages, maybe a few weeks."

She trembled with frustration at the thought she might not see him for such a long time. After the events of the previous forty-eight hours she had grown so attached to him. Her confidence had become so dependent on his physical presence; she was flabbergasted at the thought of returning to England on her own. He'd done so much for her to get her enterprise off the ground. He couldn't just abandon her now.

"Don't worry, Julia,"

His face was full of vitality and his voice fresh and firm. "I can always fly over for a weekend. I'm not going to run away, you know, or forget you. We've started something special here. It's not going to go away. You better believe it."

Her disappointment was tangible and unmistakable. He kissed her but she averted her gaze afraid to look into his eyes. She suddenly lost her appetite. Her stomach went cold and hollow. She just didn't know what to say to him. What could she say? All was said. He was staying on in Italy to accomplish his mission which, to be fair to him, he had embarked on before her arrival. She had to return home to view, rent and launch her shop in Bournemouth. What was wrong with that? They both had to pursue their own ambitions. It all made sense. But what would become of their intertwined destinies and their emotions? How could he enslave her so completely and then just walk away nonchalantly? Did he not care for her? Was he not falling in love with her as she had? Did he not need her?

"Julia, have you forgotten your exciting venture in Bournemouth?" His voice was harsh and cutting.

"I can help you from here too, you know. I don't have to hold your hand all the time."

She found his last remark demeaning and she knew it would go on tormenting her all day. She also knew emotionally at that moment she was a complete wreck. But she hoped it wouldn't affect her level of competence.

"I'll call you every day. Trust me," he said

"I do trust you", she said stiffly.

Chapter 7

It had only been a week since Julia's incredible turn of fortune in Italy. But it felt agonizingly longer. She tried to call him the moment she landed in England but his mobile was turned off. She'd left a message just to say she had landed safely thanking him for everything he had done for her. What she really wanted to tell him was that she was already missing him terribly. That the instant the jet plane soared into the Milan skyline a sickening feeling had descended to the pit of her stomach, but above all she thought she had fallen in love with him. All she got back was a brief text wishing her well and promising to call her soon. How soon he never said. But soon wasn't soon enough for Julia.

It was like slow torture as far as she was concerned. All sorts of doubts crept in to unsettle her, doubts that dented her new confidence, doubts about her sexual life and her whole being. Did he not find her as desirable and amazing anymore? Did he not miss her at all? Surely he would have called if he did. How difficult could it be to pick up the phone to say hello if you really cared? Wasn't their attraction mutual? Had their love-making not created a cocoon of exclusive intimacy around them?

Despite her own better judgement and Lindsey's nagging words of wisdom, she chose only to listen to her own little voice, resigning herself to constant torment. It was wholly disarming and so excruciatingly painful to feel unloved, deserted after the elation of so much hope and promise. She kept her mobile close to her day and night, desperately waiting for the elusive call or text. But there was nothing not even a single word from him.

Two weeks passed and still not a word from Franco. Her desperation was starting to ring alarm bells in her head threatening her sanity. She woke up feeling sore, thinking of him. She was spending most mornings lying in bed, in isolation, refusing to go out with her friends. She fought the desire to call Giuseppe at the restaurant and ask about him but was scared of even more humiliation. Her days were bleak, shrouded in agonising frustration and dejection.

Every night she dreamt of him and every second of her waking hours she thought of him. He wasn't going to go away. She craved to hear his comforting voice; his vigorous tones had filled her with so much strength and confidence. They made her feel so empowered, so full of vitality especially when he stood at her side. She allowed her thoughts to travel back to those enthralling moments their bodies had interlocked into one, when the unbearable heat of passion had sent her soaring to another galaxy on surrendering to his charm.

But one sun-drenched morning, as the warm rays caressed her cheeks, she shook off every feeling of self-pity and dejection that had ransomed her heart and her soul. She had promised herself to be strong, independent and ambitious. She had sworn she would see her little venture to the bitter end no matter what.

"For heaven's sake, get hold of yourself, Julia." It was a long overdue reprimand which sprung from her soul.

"You can't go on tormenting yourself forever."

She desperately tried to convince herself it was time to move on. Maybe it had just been a passing fancy which she had totally misinterpreted. Maybe it was just a two-night stand or maybe it was the Italian way. Whatever it was, it was over, pure and simple.

As she got up and showered her dripping body there were feelings of guilt, hatred, abhorrence, sorrow and self-pity. But she snubbed the strong temptation to fill the hollow inside her with hatred. She refused to hate him. She would hate herself first. In spite of everything he was a man of integrity. He had proven it to her.

Once she was out of the shower, she put on some light make-up and conquered her stubborn blond curls feeling better. She braced herself and was ready to face the challenges of the new day.

She briskly left the house, got into the car and started the engine.

Yet in the depths of her stomach there was still a residual emptiness nagging her. But she was adamant she wasn't going to spend the morning in a miserable mood trying to banish gloom. It would all pass, she heard herself say. It would, she reassured herself. Anyway, it was his loss. She wondered what it would be like if she accidentally bumped into him. He wasn't going to remain in Italy for ever. So he said. The probability was their paths would cross, sooner or later. A wisp of fear lingered in her mind. What would she say to him? How would her body react?

That same afternoon she went to view an empty office space right in the heart of Bournemouth. Uncannily, it had housed Estate Agents who had folded. She loved the location the moment she walked in and decided to rent it indefinitely there and then without even bothering to consult Lindsey. Only after signing the papers did she call her to give her the good news.

"Great. That's great, Julia." Lindsey was over the moon.

"When do we start?"

Julia handed in her notice at work but Lindsey preferred to stay on at the Estate Agency on a reduced workload till she knew exactly how big a part she would play in Julia's business enterprise. The next day they had the decorators in and by the weekend most of the mahogany shelving, stands, stools and banquettes of varying sizes were in place, looking exquisite in readiness for the imminent arrival of the stars themselves: The shoes.

Julia didn't have to wait long for them. Only a couple of days later as she surveyed the mail, her eyes lit up when they fell on a red card from the Parcel Post Depot announcing the arrival of a host of packages from Italy.

Her lungs almost exploded with pride. "Yes. Yes." She clenched her fists and braced herself for an enthralling day's work. She picked the phone up and called a local courier service. Within a matter of minutes a tall, fresh-faced man stood at her door. Half an hour later he returned delivering the entire order. It comprised a hundred smart white boxes each containing a pair of hand-made ladies shoes.

"Wow!" Her excitement instantly banished any thought of doom or frustration. This was exactly the medicine she needed to lift her spirits. She eagerly tore away the stubborn wrapping and started to stack the boxes one on top of the other. She opened the first box and smiled at the shimmering beige elegance staring her in the face. She picked up the shoe and ran her itching fingers over the smooth hide. Then she raised it to her nostrils and took a deep breath. The strong whiff of leather imbued her senses like a potent drug.

She couldn't resist the temptation any longer. She slipped them on and graciously paced up and down. Keeping her eyes closed she dreamt for a long moment. Her spirit soared. It was a sensation comparable to an exclusive stroll on the Milan catwalk in the company of glamour, opulence and fame.

When her eyelids lifted, the catwalk feeling stayed with her but without the opulence and the celebrity audience. Nonetheless, it was a nice feeling making her really proud of herself. This was a decision she would never regret. Who knows, maybe this was the best route to prosperity, fame and fortune, and why not happiness? She sighed and then proceeded to open the second box and the third and the fourth until it was time for a short coffee break.

Time to call Lindsey, she told herself. She would be ecstatic when she saw the exclusive range of shoes ready to bedeck every stand and shelf in her chic boutique.

She certainly was when she walked into the shop that afternoon.

"Why didn't you call me earlier?" she complained. "I was on tenterhooks."

"They only just arrived this morning, Lindsey. I've only just seen them myself."

Julia was delighted Lindsey loved them too; she would be the first to notice anything out of place, unsuitable or damaged. Her stamp of approval was definitely the highest praise possible. To Julia it was like a royal blessing.

"Let's open them all."

"No, no, calm down, Lindsey. I don't want a mess all over the place. I'd rather put them out, a few at a time. I want to get the display right with the minimal look. We don't want to confuse the shoppers."

Although she treasured Lindsey's help and opinion she knew her weakness. Her exuberance sometimes ran away with her. So she had to keep a close eye on her and restrain her moments of endemic impatience.

"This is going to be a huge success, you know." Lindsey's face was incandescent. "I know it."

"I hope so after all efforts I've put into it." Unease crept upon her face. Her voice quivered. "And a lot of money most of which is a bank loan, I hasten to add."

"True." Lindsey was a little taken aback at the unexpected apprehension tainting Julia's tone of voice. She couldn't help notice the expiring flames in her eyes. Just when she was about to ask if Franco was still on her mind and in her life, she immediately knew the answer.

As they set about opening more boxes, deliberating on the choice of place for each shoe, it was obvious Julia's heart was somewhere else. Wherever it was, it certainly wasn't there in the shop. For the first time in her life she was speechless. She just didn't know what to say to her. She knew how sensitive and vulnerable Julia could be and probably more so now since her Italian adventure (or misadventure, she thought).

"When is your next delivery then?" She asked instead holding her breath.

"I don't know. Probably next week, I guess." Julia spoke curtly, void of her customary vitality, just responding to every question without much rational thought or passion.

"You know, you're going to need a proper shop assistant soon." It was becoming desperately hard engaging her in any sort of rational conversation. Lindsey hoped she wouldn't construe her comment as a form of nagging. She just wanted to help. Julia herself had frequently admitted that her words were like gold to her. She respected her opinions. But Lindsey was starting to have serious doubts now.

Julia simply frowned seemingly unable to respond to the suggestion. She swung her head like a lazy pendulum contemplating the possibilities while staring wistfully at the white shoe snugly resting on the glass stand. Then she turned and looked askance at Lindsey:

"Would you like the job?"

"Oh, I'd love it Julia. I thought you'd never ask. But don't you think I deserve a better title than shop assistant?" she teased trying to take Julia's mind away from whatever was troubling her.

"Well, you can always call yourself manager." There was a hint of a smile on her lips bringing untold relief to Lindsey's taut nerves.

"Or partner, maybe."

"Julia I'm dying to be a part of it but not sure about partner. It sounds like a lot of responsibility to me. It's your money, your baby for heaven's sake." The relief in Lindsey's voice was tangible. At least she had coaxed her into a normal string of exchanges.

"You know you can always count on me. I'll always be there for you as a non-descript personnel to help or nag you as the case might be." It sounded a mistimed gamble but it worked a treat. This time it was a fully constituted grin that puffed up Julia's cheeks lifting some of the misery. It seemed like a ray of sunshine had just filtered through the shop window brightening the prospects for the rest of the day.

"You need someone stable in here so you won't be tied up yourself all day. And I hope you're going to get yourself a decent accountant too."

"I've already thought of that. It's under control." Her weary mood seemed to have lifted and her mind was wholly focused on the immediate present. Lindsey's effervescence evidently had played its part. It was at searing junctures like these when she felt most grateful for their friendship. "What would I do without you?" She hugged her tightly for a long spell.

It was such a huge relief to have a friend like her. If she had gone with her to Italy, then maybe she would have exercised better control over herself. But she didn't want to go there again. In a determined attempt to banish the thought she quickly picked up a shoe for no particular reason and kept turning it over in the palm of her hand.

"Not much." chirped Lindsey.

They both laughed at themselves. "But then where would I be without you?"

In the days when Lindsey herself had just come out of a long relationship which devastated her, driving her to excessive drinking and suicidal attempts, it was none other than Julia, who single-handedly had practically picked her up from her already dug up grave, shook her out of her woeful dereliction and patiently nursed her to complete rehabilitation.

She had missed work erratically for a whole month on her account but never was there a word of complaint on her lips. She did it all out of her devotion and loyalty to her friend because she knew then if the tables turned Lindsey would do the same. How thankful she was for such a special bond, a friendship made in heaven if indeed there was one. Maybe there was a God after all, she smiled at the unfamiliar but serene thought.

"I'm so thankful you're always there when I need you. I don't think I'd have done this if I hadn't been sure of your support."

"Of course you could." Lindsey's face was a huge frown.

"When you set your mind to something Julia, you always deliver. And you know it. Anyway, you never listen to anything I say because if you did you would be the new Adele.

Colour by now was completely restored to her cheeks. Her weariness had mitigated. She was now in a much better mood to face the rest of the day. "By the way, have I told you yet?"

"Told me what?" A keen anticipation burnt in Lindsey's face, her ears pricked up and her painted eyelids revealed huge brown eyes.

"I finally have a name for the shop. I'm going to call it Grace". Her smoky eyes held a glint of deep satisfaction. She had spent sleepless nights turning over long lists of possible names, stylish names some of which had unfortunately already been taken like 'Scruples' and 'Chic' and 'The Italian Job'. But 'Grace' she thought would be perfect. She had decided on it when she opened the first box and felt the shoes purring in her hands. All she saw was shimmering gracefulness smiling at her. It didn't take her long.

"Grace … just Grace?" Lindsey was not at all impressed. She did not think Grace was very original for a stylish specialist shop like Julia's. She was expecting something more eye catching, more sensational, more original. Something that would fizz in your mouth, spread like wildfire and have the whole city talking about it. But

Grace, just Grace fell flat on its face. Why not 'Cinderella's' or 'Shoes with Attitude' or something with more modern appeal she wondered.

"You know what?" A bright spark flickered in Julia's eyes. Her tone was crisp and confident.

"What?" Lindsey asked.

"Just Grace, how about 'Just Grace', I love it."

Lindsey listened to the sound of it and instantly decided she loved it too. They laughed gleefully, hugged each other and danced around the room while passers-by looked on bemused and pretended to join in the merriment.

"This calls for a celebration." Lindsey's joy suddenly spilled over and a thesaurus of ideas dazzled through her head. She picked up her phone and started calling the long list of regular partygoers.

"Just Grace," Julia repeated over and over. "How weird was that?" She shook her head with a permanent huge smile covering her face.

"There was I spending sleepless nights and coming up with nothing. Then you walk in and a few minutes later the most original of name crops up, just like that."

"They call it team work." she said, interrupting her conversation on the phone.

"I couldn't have come up with that all by myself." Two heads always better than one, Julia thought. How she would have liked Lindsey to join her full time in her venture as a full partner. They would make a formidable team. It would be so much more fun than doing it all by herself. She didn't have anything else to prove to herself now. She'd already done a huge amount successfully when she went to Italy to order the stuff, finding and renting the place and organising everything in her head. She'd done the difficult groundwork, granted with a bit of help from Franco and his friends. She couldn't deny that. The sheer thought of him sent a slithering ache to her stomach which she pretended to ignore. This was a time for joy not regret. That was history now. What really mattered were the present and more importantly, the future. As things stood, the future looked very bright at that moment.

The desire to seriously ask Lindsey again to partner her lingered on in her heart all night. She decided to wait for a more opportune moment before she would face her with her formal request. It wasn't going to be easy, she knew. Lindsey preferred a more happy-go-lucky approach to life and a liberal, go-as-you-please attitude. That would be a death-toll for any business. But she could change with the right incentive and motivation.

The venue picked by Lindsey's guests for the celebratory evening was Poole. Julia couldn't have been more disappointed. They could have asked her in the first place but she wasn't going to kick up a fuss. The plan was to gradually trek the coast exploring a variety of top clubs. Their first stop was a hip Wine bar extremely popular with the younger generation. These frequently congregated outside in huddles and drank boisterously till the early hours.

"This is to Julia." Lindsey raised her first Vodka inviting the rest of them to follow suit.

"To Julia." the rest of them endorsed.

"To Julia." sang a chorus of vibrant, baritone voices from the other side of the bar. A raucous cheer broke out. The girls had caught the keen attention of a group of men, most tall and stocky, possibly rugby players who suddenly decided to liven up Julia's party. "Speech, speech." they entreated, "We want a speech, Julia."

Julia's face went red as a beet and her arms were covered in goose-bumps. The hair on her neck stood up while her throat dried up. She sunk in her sparkling new *stivaletti* pretending not to hear anything.

"Speech, speech Julia." cried another voice.

Lindsey looked at her almost entreatingly.

"I'm not giving a speech. Just ignore them. They're all probably a little tipsy, anyway." she finally spat out. "But if they want to buy me a drink I wouldn't say no."

"Go on Julia, just a short one."

At that moment a tall, dark hunk extended his long beefy arm to her and handed over an Iced Vodka.

"Happy Birthday Julia, this is from the lads." He planted a big wet kiss on her cheek.

The girls took it as a cue for another hearty cheer. Within seconds Julia's name was on everyone's lips in the pub.

"If this goes on in every pub", hooted one of the girls, "your name will make headlines tomorrow morning." Crackles of laughter rose above the loud conversations and the continuous jingle of glasses.

It didn't take long for the alcohol to peak as the girls staggered to the next pub, a few metres up the road. Some were already unsteady on their feet, swinging sideways singing all sorts of mumbo-jumbo. After a half dozen Vodkas, a few Schnapps and Sambucas for good measure, the evening was ready to swing into a lively main event at a night club.

"I don't know about you lot", crackled another girl. "But I feel like a Chinese. Who's for a little nosh-up?"

"I've got a better suggestion", cried another. "I say we go the full hog and go Italian." Looking at her watch, she went on. "They'll still be serving if we hurry up."

At the sound of the word Italian Julia's heart sank to the pits. The evening had been a total blast so far and she was grateful to all the girls for their amazing support. But something told her this was the moment to make a sharp exit or she might regret the entire evening. Lindsey closely observed her reaction from the corner of her eyes and instantly knew it was a bad idea.

"Oh, I don't know." She skimmed every face looking for allies. "I'm dying to hit the dance floor myself."

"Oh, unless I get some grub into this body now, I'm going to collapse like a pregnant cow. I can assure you it won't be a pretty sight, I'm telling you."

There was little Lindsey could do to save Julia's day as most of the girls warmed to the idea of food. The liberal flow of alcohol in their blood had so debilitated them; some had to be helped into the waiting taxis.

"I'm sorry girls", said Julia acidly. "It's been a blast, but my body needs some proper rest. It's been a long day for me and it's an early start tomorrow. Thank you for a wonderful evening everyone and watch your waistline."

"Sod the waistline." garbled a distant croak. "I can murder a Margherita."

"Oh, come on Julia. You know the hunky waiter fancies you."

Lindsey was about to excuse herself and hop out of the taxi. She couldn't let Julia leave on her own. It was like an implicit treaty between them to stick together through thick and thin. A sense of duty compelled her to accompany her.

"Lindsey." Julia was quick to counter. "I'll be okay. You go with the girls and have fun. I'll call you tomorrow."

"I can't let you go on your own."

"Yes, you can, Lindsey. I'll be okay. I insist. You go with the girls."

"You're sure?" Lindsey squinted at her.

"Yes, I'm sure." She shut the door of the taxi, waved them goodbye and jumped into the next one.

The following morning after an overdue lie-in, Lindsey found herself tormented by an enormous dilemma. What a godsend it had been Julia had left when she did. They had eventually settled for the Bergamese restaurant. Sitting not far from their table was the Italian Stallion himself, Franco and he had female company.

It was a beautiful Mediterranean–looking woman, definitely older than Julia, probably in her late forties with the looks of a model half her age. Long shimmering dark curls framed a flawless face with large, beautiful hazel eyes, a tanned body to die for and long slim legs proud enough to grace a Milan catwalk. She wore a sober black satin dress and spoke very little. She was the main event and completely eclipsed the handsome, breezy waiter.

What was she to do? She sat dolefully all morning and into the afternoon. If she told Julia it would break her heart again and she'd only just recovered, if that. Maybe she hadn't recovered at all considering how she reacted the previous night. She was terrified of unexpectedly facing

Franco in Poole and who wouldn't be after getting so close to him, then getting so callously dumped?

The dilemma afflicting her was like a two-edged sword. If she chose not to tell her, it would be tantamount to a betrayal and she couldn't do that. Yet it would be the best solution, probably the only way to protect Julia from feeling sorry for herself.

If Julia ever found out the truth about the previous night it would destroy her and her glamour business venture would go up in flames. It would crush her soul to the point of no recovery. What then? How could she ever live with the enormous guilt of Julia's demise or forgive herself? The thought of it alone was unbearable. There was no winning formula available to her. But choose she had to, for the frustrating torment of sitting in the middle was killing her. But how was she going to decide?

Damage limitation seemed the best criteria and the only way she could adopt. If she chose not to tell her and then found out through other channels Julia would never forgive her. Sooner or later, words were bound to slip out gratuitously out of the mouth of one of the girls. So Julia was bound to find out irrespective of what Lindsey wanted. Now that made her decision so much easier.

That afternoon she drove to Bournemouth and popped into Julia's shop. Julia was busy putting the finishing touches before the approaching opening day. She had decided to forego all the glitz she had planned and opt for the unceremonious opening. She thought the shop didn't need any fancy opening night. The shoes were the main all-conquering protagonists and could speak for themselves. They didn't need endorsing by any dazzling D.J. or showbiz celebrity. So, all she did was to advertise the opening night on bill-boards, newspapers and the local radio. It didn't cost her much and would do the job equally efficiently.

"Lindsey." Julia was in a cheerful mood. "Just the person." she bawled. She was about to tell her about the opening of her boutique "Just Grace". And she had only just received another large consignment from Italy.

"Julia. You look great."

"Thank you. So do you. I can't wait to show you my latest arrivals. They are something else, Lindsey." She quickly disappeared into the stock room and came back carrying two boxes.

"Julia. I've something to tell you."

"Oh, that can wait. You've to see these little babies first. They're just amazing. Honestly, you've never seen anything like them. I promise."

"Julia." Her voice was harsh. "This is important and I've to tell you now before I change my mind."

"Oh?" Julia looked shocked. Her jaw fell and her eyes popped out. "What is it then? Are you alright?"

"Yes, I'm fine. It's …. euh … It's Franco." Her tone was now soft and silky and almost numb.

"Franco? What about Franco?" Julia's face fell and her heart stopped beating.

"I'm sorry but I've to tell you this, Julia. I'd never forgive myself if I didn't. And neither would you."

"Has he done something? Has he been involved in an accident? What is it, Lindsey?" Her blood surged and her head ached.

"Are you going to tell me then?"

"Franco was at the restaurant last night."

"So he's back? Good. It is his restaurant. I don't understand why this is so important. Did he ask for me?" Julia's harsh tones betrayed anger and frustration.

"Julia."

Icy, white-faced and numbed by an intense agony, Julia had stopped to breathe. The growing torment was unbearable. Why was Lindsey being so mean and brutal? What was the point of her delaying tactics? But she didn't want to lose her calm. It could betray the fact she still had feelings for him. She simply stared at her desperately fighting a smouldering fury inside her. If Lindsey ever sensed she still harboured feelings for him she would break down and become an inconsolable wreck.

"What, what is it, Lindsey? Are you going to tell me because I can't read your mind, can I?"

"I'm sorry Julia. But this is so difficult for me. Please understand me. It hurts me as much as it will hurt you."

"Well, why don't you just spell it out then? You're making me a bag of nerves and I can't bear it any longer." A film of sweat covered her forehead.

"Franco had female company." She said mournfully and paused. "He was sitting with a beautiful woman. I think she was Italian, in her forties, maybe an ex-model."

"An ex-model and how would you know? What do you know about Italian models? Or ex-models for that matter" Her face grudgingly twisted into an angry knot.

"Maybe she was his sister. Sisters can be beautiful too."

"Julia, something told me she wasn't. I wish she was for your sake and mine. But it looked like something much more intimate. Not like having a cosy conversation with your sister."

Julia stood silent, downcast and vulnerable. Her hands were cold and the sweat on her forehead had chilled. She felt like a solitary iceberg ebbing away into a cold, uncaring ocean.

"Believe me, Julia. I agonised all morning over this but there was no other way. What else could I do? I know I haven't done a good job the way I told it, but … you know me. I'm a nervous wreck myself and I can't believe I actually told you. I was shivering before I walked in here and prayed I wouldn't burst out crying," she carried on now her welled up eyes streaming down her cheeks.

Julia held her closely in her arms.

"I'm sorry. I didn't mean to be so hard on you. That was rude. You are such a gem and I'm so lucky to have you as my friend." She hugged her lingeringly and both shared tears.

"Thank you." She said huskily. "I know how hard it must have been for you to tell me."

"Will you be okay?"

"Do I have a choice?" her brows lifted. Her voice was distant. Then after a long, pensive moment, "I guess it had to happen sooner or later. I just have to be strong."

She had to resign herself to the tricky new situation and hope it didn't destroy her. Life was always full of difficult twists and turns. She should have known it when she let him into her life.

"But it's my problem now, not yours." She conjured up a semblance of a smile.

"No, Julia. It's our problem. Remember I'm the one who introduced you to him."

"Don't be silly, Lindsey."

"No, I mean it. You stood by my side when I needed you. And I'll be there for you in your time of tribulations," She added.

"It's very sweet of you and I'm grateful. But this is a situation I've to deal with myself, in my own way. If I don't I'll regret it. I hope you understand."

Julia realised then the terrible mistake she did accepting Franco's help in her business venture. It had sadly completely eclipsed the joy of it all, including her dream. It hugely devalued her input which had been no mean effort by any standards. It exposed her to his capricious patronage for the rest of her life. She had thoughtlessly allowed herself to become one of his many conquests and now she was paying the price.

Her foolish heart seemed unable to shake off the fetters hampering her every breath. Unless she succeeded in breaking the chain enslaving her body for his awesome figure, then all her endeavours, her dreams, her newly gained confidence would all have been in vain. Her long-awaited successes would all go up in smoke. It wouldn't be much of a life, just a tedious litany of little deeds and a whole lot of mediocrity. Something had to be done and quite soon. But what exactly?

That evening she decided everything was in place for the imminent opening. She took a deep sigh of relief and satisfaction, picked up her handbag and the keys and was about to lock up. Suddenly, out of thin air, loomed a tall dark shadow at the entrance to the shop.

Chapter 8

"Hello Julia."

It was the same dark familiar tone that had scooped her away into the land of dreams in Milan, a tone which had flitted through all her defences like wild fire burning remorselessly inside her.

"How are you?"

His indrawn breath gave away a sense of excitement that rarely ruffled his surface. His jet-black lashes lifted as did his angular jaws.

"I missed you."

It was only then she realised how much she had missed him. A feeling of immense delight soared through her all her body. Her heart beat with growing ruthlessness, snubbing her every resolution for the umpteenth time.

"Franco", she sighed, breathing heavily and shaking.

"What are you doing here? How did you find me?"

"Haven't you missed me?" He queried.

That was the last question she wanted to answer or could answer. Her shaking faded instead stubborn stabs sliced through her body making any sort of rational response ever more difficult. He had caught her so unawares, so terribly unprepared she just didn't know what to say or do next.

"Where have you been? You didn't call me not even once."

I hate you, her heart screamed out but not loud enough. It wasn't a hateful hate, of the type that bears deep loathing. This was different. It was a loving hate between lovers, a slap on the wrist admonishing a moment of impetuosity but continuing loving soon after. There was a dark, magnetic pull behind his blue-eyed charm which she had always found hard to resist. How could she if her body kept on sending her mixed signals? She wanted to hate him, to slap, not just his wrist but his cheek too. But deep down, the floods of crushing sensations were telling her otherwise. They were unstoppable and unbearable. But her initial hateful rage was absurdly replaced by an intense hunger of a terrifying compulsion to touch him, to hold him close to her once again and to feel his powerful grip. Only that could calm her down.

"Why didn't you call?"

The words had hardly left her lips when he gripped her quite brutally and kissed her on the cupid's bow of her mouth. She gasped, struggling not to kiss him back until their lips parted. But why did she keep pushing him away? She turned her head and retreated.

"You think you can just walk in here and expect me to welcome you with open arms? Does it not even cross your mind the pain you've inflicted on me? First you seduce me, oh what a real gent you were, a knight in shining armour and then you dump me as if I didn't exist anymore.

Well, I've got news for you..... Get lost."

The mist in her eyes grew but a huge lump was off her chest. She swallowed and caught her breath again. Relieved she had the courage and strength to release the torrent of mixed emotions inside her, enough to defend her dignity, she found herself reduced to an uncomfortable silence. She stood there defiantly in front of him, unable to look him in his eyes.

"I am sorry, Julia." His tense eyes fought to lock on to hers.

"I put my hands up, I deserve this. I'm not very good at phoning or texting. Never been and never will be, I'm afraid. I'd rather have a face to face conversation, in case I say the wrong thing then I'm able to put it right there and then."

"Oh, and that's your excuse?" Her voice was fiercer. She shrugged holding her belligerent pose, her hands stapled to her sides.

"I knew you'd be in Bournemouth town centre, anyway I saw your car parked outside." He exposed a mouthful of pearls but no smile came across to her. "I'll make it up to you, Julia. You'll see."

"No, you won't." she snapped more brittle and icy than a Siberian winter.

"And what makes you think I'm such an easy prey?"

She instantly sensed her truculent strategy was getting her nowhere. His wealth of confidence and steely resilience was not in the least unruffled.

"Why did you take me to your posh villa and make love to me if.....?

"If what? You don't think I meant it?" His eyes did not leave her face for a single minute. "You don't think I actually care for you?" He lifted his chin revealing faint throbbing in his throat. The abrasive skin of his neck was so taut the muscles beneath jumped out. "I missed you too, you know."

"Who said I missed you?" The mist in her darkened green eyes belied her sharp words. "And I don't believe you missed me at all."

"That's not fair, Julia. And you know it. You weren't just a passing fancy. You're much more than that. You've done something to me no other woman could do.

That's why I had to make love to you because I truly wanted you. Is that so hard to understand?" He took a deep breath pacing around staring at the catwalk of splendid shoes. An insolent smile danced fleetingly on his tight lips. His voice was now remote and toneless.

Perhaps her petulance was finally getting to him. She detected an ambiguous spark in his eyes. Was it a spark of wonderment maybe? Was he about to acknowledge her awesome achievement? Not likely, she thought. The Franco she knew would sooner take off on a trip in self-righteousness underlying his satisfaction at his considerable contribution to her venture.

Julia had no ready response. She was finding him insufferable.

"It's just lust. All is lust for you not love." she spurted out mockingly, wallowing at the aptness of her response.

"Was it lust for you?"

She was not expecting that. The longer this went on, the less reassuring and frustrating she was finding it all. She had no idea where all this was leading to. Her confidence was as battered as it had ever been. Of course, it hadn't been lust for her. He had swept her off her feet. Any idiot could see that. She had admitted to herself, she had fallen in love with him. Her body had never before experienced such delirious pleasure. He had won her over despite all the formidable defences she had put up to fight him off.

"Was it?" His jaws tightened.

"Franco, don't."

She would have clutched at anything to keep her composure. But she wasn't going to answer because she knew she couldn't win. Either way he would have another lofty argument up his sleeve. She did not want to lie to him. No, it wasn't lust to her. Her heart was well and truly entangled. But what could she say? What else was there to draft in for her defence?

"Is this why you came here?"

"No Julia, you're wrong." His eyes smiled mockingly.

"I came here to take you out to dinner and pick up where we left off."

"Where we left off? Where you left off you mean." The hurt in her voice touched him.

"Well the answer is no thank you."

"Julia, you can't mean it?"

"Well, I do," she snapped.

Her heart kept pounding, while her mind refusing to be convinced. But within seconds, she was starting to regret her curt response.

"Julia, give me a chance. It's just a little setback, that's all." The conviction in his voice was firm.

"It's not as if I deserted you for another?"

"No?" Searing flames suddenly burnt in her eyes, her heart froze and chest flared up.

"Tell me then. Who was the fancy Bimbo at your restaurant you were dining with last night? Was it your sister or your mother? Or was it your daughter?" Her voice roared like a wronged lioness's slicing through him with the chilling precision of a seasoned surgeon.

"Julia, listen." he commanded. "I can explain everything if you let me."

"Can you?"

"Yes, there is a perfectly good explanation. The morning you left Milan I got some bad news."

"I don't really want to listen to this Franco." Julia was convinced if she dallied a second longer he would twist her round his little finger again and all her daring resistance would have been in vain. When was she going to learn to be less vulnerable and more ruthless? Now was the time to put her foot down, end of story. Her better judgement told her to lock up, say goodbye to him and go home alone. That shouldn't be too difficult for her? So why was she still standing in front of him, listening to him? Had she forgotten his azure gaze had hypnotic powers? Why was she allowing her untutored heart to dither, exposing herself once again to his guile? He'd dumped her. He had deserted her and embarked on another conquest. What more proof did she need to send him packing there and then?

Yet how incredulous could she be? A few minutes later, she was sitting with him sipping a coffee at the café Rouge not far from the beach. Was she out of her mind? She must have been. Why else would she have allowed herself yet again to be wheedled into the shadow of his magical spell? Why had she accepted to get into his car and let him drive her to the café? She had nothing to say to him anyway and had no intention of listening to his pack of lies.

Obviously, he was pink with pleasure as he sat across the table dotingly. The café was not busy. There was only one other couple at the next table having a coffee and croissants. The wall behind them was hung by matt burgundy wallpaper punctuated with what seemed like a host of large mushrooms. The spotlight above them lit up the white ceiling which suspended a glowing halo over their table.

For a long moment Julia refused to even look at him. She languidly pored over the wallpaper then, almost in fascination regaled in the couple who held hands across the table. The man was probably in his late forties, thin on top but his date, a very pretty brunette in a perfect bob maybe just turned thirty. They seemed totally absorbed in one another, whispering little sweet nothings. They interrupted their *tête-à-tête* for a short second, smiled politely at her and Franco then duly returned to their cosy bubble of intimacy.

"So? I'm all ears." she said sternly, not knowing what on earth she was doing there. She wasn't really interested in anything he had to say to her. But what else could she say to lift the ailing conversation? She turned her gaze away once again, nowhere in particular. She smiled lingeringly at the girl and started to count the mushrooms on the wall, next glanced broodingly at a distant Picasso print, fiddling playfully with her teaspoon. She struggled to avoid the eagle eyes deliberately scrutinising her eyeballs in silence. He was in no hurry to speak, clearly shrewdly weighing up every word for its honeyed texture. But no way would he succeed. She was not open to persuasion. Her mind was made up.

"Stop staring at me and say something?" She said heavily, her eyes daring him to even try and convince her.

"If not I'm just going to walk out. Anyway, I don't know why I came here. It was a stupid idea."

"Julia." His head lowered as his jaw protruded.

"My brother Giuseppe died in a traffic accident the same day you left Milan." He spat out in a heavy and restrained voice.

She shrugged in shock and froze unable to utter a single word. Her heart stopped beating, her stomach slumped to her feet and her lips refused to move. All she could do was close tightly her aching eyes and sigh in silence. Her dry throat was killing her.

"How?" she heard herself croak pathetically.

"He had come over to help me find a charming location for a new restaurant. A friend of ours was driving when a lorry just ahead of them was heavily leaking diesel. They lost control and skidded right under the lorry. Their car caught fire and they both burnt to death."

"Oh my God, I'm sorry Franco....... I'm so sorry," she finally managed to let out.

Disbelief and embarrassment spread across her face. She grasped his hand that stretched out across the table, squeezed it against her cheek. She could hardly breathe. What a terrible tragedy. There she was insulting him most of the evening after all he had done for her when all he needed was a warm embrace and solace.

"I'm really sorry, Franco. I didn't know." She quickly stumbles to her feet, walks around the table and held him tightly in her arms. They stood locked together for a long moment. She felt so privileged to share what must have been an agonising experience.

At difficult moments like this words were of no practical use. Nothing she could say would lift his overwhelming grief. Sorry seemed to be the only word she could think of but it was so inadequate, so utterly futile and impersonal. Surely there had to be some other magical word, maybe in Italian or French or some other biblical language that could touch his heart, lighten the burden crushing his soul.

I wish I'd have been there with you." she finally said, her unsteady voice softer than a whisper.

"Thank you." He took a deep slow breath and caressed the small of her back with the palm of his hand. "It means a lot to me, Julia."

Even at this awkward moment Julia was dying to find out who the mysterious lady in black was.

"So, are you going to tell me who that pretty lady was with you at your restaurant?"

"Julia, that pretty lady who I had dinner with last night is Giuseppe's wife. Well, widow now."

He then serrated his lips and she sensed a sea of love flooding his eyes. It took him a few seconds to compose himself and pick up where he left.

"She is inconsolable and who can blame her? Giuseppe was an absolute darling, a saint if there ever was one. There wasn't anything he wouldn't do to make her happy which she was, believe me. To add to that he was the perfect brother to me, the best friend you can ever have. Just a great human being you were proud of knowing." He spoke in a hard, sad voice. "He was a top chef too." His mouth gave a humourless smile.

"What a loss it must be for both of you." she awkwardly continued.

"There wasn't a dry eye at his funeral. If he could see the large crowd of mourners that turned up he wouldn't have believed they were there for him. It's ironic isn't it; only after your death do you get to find who your real friends are." His voice was austere, almost bitter. "Well, life must go on. Feeling bitter the rest of your days is not worth it. Giuseppe would have wanted her to carry on being happy in his fond memory. I don't think she has a single picture of him lacking a huge smile on his face. Even as kids in Italy, he was always smiling. I remember when his dog died. We buried it in the garden and he came up with this little song for it...... May you go up to heaven dancing and laughing. Believe it or not the dog used to seem to laugh with him. I know it sounds balmy but it was true. You had to see it to believe it. He called it 'Pagliaccio'. That's Italian for clown."

"How sweet," she said diffidently.

A warm smile invaded his face for in a way he had atoned to his unpardonable desertion. He hoped she didn't wallow in recriminations, but forgiveness, so they could pick up where they had left off.

The café was steadily filling up when they paid and rose to leave. It had been a totally unexpected and wholly surreal meeting, once more throwing her life in turmoil. She had experienced every feeling in the book from anger to revenge, exasperation to apathy, then shock, sympathy and sorrow together with anguish and love. At last hope had relit a shimmering glow in her heart. But it had been like having four seasons in one day.

Sitting next to him in the car, she felt completely drained and impassive, unable to think of any useful words to console him. She didn't want to distress him by asking more questions about Giuseppe. Even though it seemed to bring joy to his blue eyes, talking about his childhood days in Italy, their adventures by the river Adda in the summer and their memorable visits to the mountains in the winter.

"Will you keep me company today?" he asked looking at her with an odd mix of pride and sadness in his eyes. The desire in them grew the more he stared at her, but it wasn't a lustful desire, it was an honest craving of the child in him, a craving straight from the soul for motherly affection. How he hoped she would not say no. She didn't have it in her to be cruel to him.

Yet a voice within her warned her to keep silent. She couldn't avert her look away from the mask of pain hanging over his face. His usual glow had dwindled away. It was a pain she made hers. So she stared at him lovingly, afraid to shut her eyes or speak. "Will you? Is that a yes?" he asked stiffly.

Uneasily, wondering how the day was going to end, she desperately tried to persuade herself to do the honourable thing. She had forgiven him, which was the easy bit. But there was a vast labyrinth of conflicting feelings playing havoc inside her. She couldn't decide what to listen to or follow. She sensed it wasn't going to be a straightforward yes or no. It never is and a yes couldn't exactly mean they could forget everything, wave the magic wand and return in a happy flashback to the blissful lovemaking by his exquisite Milan pool. Things just weren't as simple as before, were they?

His eyes didn't leave her. At this point she was getting worried he might hit the car in front of them which had started to gradually slow down.

"Franco, he's slowing down." She looked at him concealing her fear.

"I know. I noticed." he said savagely. "So, will you?" he said more soberly.

"I don't know if it's a good idea" she replied wearily. "I've got so much to do, Franco and I've to pick up my car."

"You don't have to do anything, honestly. Just stay with me and keep me company. That's all I ask."

Despite the honesty in his voice there was an underlying firmness which frightened her. What if he abandoned her again and disappeared without a trace somewhere in Italy? What then? She didn't think she could cope with it. In fact she was sure she wouldn't. She needed some sort of guarantee from him, maybe sign a contract or something, promising her he would not desert her again. But he couldn't do that, could he?

She was starting to realise how successful restaurateurs were nomadic creatures by nature, endemic opportunists whose one goal in life was affluence, power and prestige. Franco was no different. No one could change him not even she, in fact least of all herself. Yet every time their eyes met she melted away like dew at sunrise. Deep down she knew she had fallen in love with him even though she kept denying it.

"I wouldn't ask if I didn't really need you, Julia."

"It's not that I don't trust you, Franco." Someone else would have probably dumped him and ran. Her face made it perfectly clear she meant every word she said. After his shocking revelations which had shaken her to the core, she felt she was learning to read him much better. Yes, she felt she could trust him now, he was not the problem. She was. It was herself she couldn't trust. She never seemed to know how she would respond to any situation. Already she was feeling the numbing effect of his powerful sway. Every time he ran his charm over her, her heart helplessly lost a beat, sending unfamiliar stabs and aches to her body.

"But I don't think it's a good idea today. Truly I don't." She carried on.

It brought immense relief to her once she got it off her chest. Franco gave her a vacant look and carried on driving regardless. She sensed beneath his serene state lay concealed a sea of disappointment and angst. The residual grief at the tragic loss of his brother, of course made it worse. After all he was only human. Franco's earlier confession had just unlocked the padlock to a dangerous dark zone ruthlessly swamped by a collection of disappointments, failures and anxieties. She looked at his angular profile, shuddered and turned her head away with a flurry of sharp twinges in her stomach.

God she thought, engulfed by a crushing emotion somewhere between disbelief and fear. It sapped whatever energy was left in her. Then echoes of Milan returned to assail her. She realised she had never really stopped missing him and nothing could fill the enormous void he had left in her soul. Not even her scintillating celebrity shoes.

Since Milan, every dream every thought had Franco as its inevitable protagonist. There wasn't one single morning she didn't wake up lying next to his ubiquitous ghost. It had become such an unshakeable obsession where sometimes she truly believed he was lying next to her. She would actually touch his face and arms, kiss his cheek, getting a whiff of his aftershave and savour his rasping skin.

Franco left the avenue, accelerated up a steep hill and turned into a slick driveway, flanked by beautifully maintained lawns. He eventually came to a stop beside a lush circular flowerbed with a feisty water-jet in the centre leaping to the second floor balcony.

"You must come in for a drink at least", he commanded as he got out, walked around to her door without even waiting for her answer.

"I didn't know you had a house in Bournemouth too." She said looking aghast and sat motionless in the car as he held her door.

"Well, long story. I almost bought a restaurant here a couple of years ago for an ex. We thought we'd run it together so I got us this house first." Pokerfaced, he spoke in a matter-of-fact way. "But it didn't work out."

"Only a quick one then", she muttered eventually getting out of his car. Common sense told her she was playing with fire. This was a foolish thing to do because in his sensitive condition with all the anguish he'd been through, his soul would certainly be crying out for more than just comforting company. Having starved his body for so long, she could tell, he was ravenous.

"I'm serious Franco just a quick one."

She knew she was talking to the wall and literally walked straight into the fire. Her instinct told her the moment she stepped inside the tastefully decorated lounge she would be at the mercy of his uncontrollable sexual prowess. His magnetism would neutralise her defences to hunger for his magical touch. She was already shaking when she nervously pulled out her cell phone from her handbag. All fingers and thumbs she started to dial for a taxi.

"This is a bad idea, I've to go."

"Please don't, Julia." He begged her.

"I really need you to be with me. I haven't stopped mourning my brother and it's been a hell of a battering. The grief got much worse after the funeral, you know. They say it gets worse before it gets better. Whether it ever gets better, of course is another matter." His voice was harsh. "Only God knows how I've missed you. I know you missed me too. Your eyes don't lie, do they?"

He got hold of her phone, placed it on the coffee table and gently held her face between the palms of his hands. He kissed her. As she tasted his kiss, she shrugged, gulped to moisten her dry throat. The last thing she wanted to do was to abandon him in his time of desperate need. She just couldn't do it to him, leave him so unfeelingly. She would have never forgiven herself for such a callous and cowardly deed.

He was a good man, undeniably arrogant, single-minded and a touch overbearing but nonetheless a good man with rarest qualities. He obviously liked her a lot and she couldn't deny the same feelings towards him. In fact deeply in love she was with him.

Every waking hour she spent thinking of him. He had filled her life with joy when he was close and when he was far. But she had also spent horrific weeks despairing. Now he was here, he had come back to her. He had the decency to make an honourable, heartrending confession for his unfortunate absence. What else could he do to convince her he was genuinely sorry? He too had missed her and hoped things would now be different.

"Julia." A semblance of a smile stretched the edges of his mouth. "Don't go." His tone was crisp and firm. This was not a weak entreaty but a command. Any other lesser man would have begged but not Franco. Despite the desperation weighing on his heart he kept his poise and dignity.

She couldn't rally enough voice to speak, for the taste of his ardent kiss had rendered her dizzy. A kiss was never just a kiss, she thought. He had taught her that himself. She slowly savoured its magic working through her veins, promising more scorching pleasure to come.

"There must be a small part of you which feels some empathy for me surely. Isn't there?" Surveying her judiciously he handed her a crystal glass lit up with a generous measure of Cognac. His face dropped as he gave a soft, cynical snigger. "Did I really hurt you so much? Have I done so much damage to you?" He shook his head in disbelief, pulled her to him quite brutally, grasped the nape of her neck and kissed her on her mouth. "Kiss me, Julia. Give me a proper kiss."

She pushed him away, ingested a crisp gulp of Cognac which burnt her throat then put her glass down and closed her eyes panic-stricken. Without even a thought, she then threw her arms around his neck and drew a sharp excited breath. She wanted him so much, her whole body arched and stiffened like a bow. Her radiant emerald eyes tugged into his hungry look. She felt a sudden, uncontrollable urge to kiss him and surrender to his fierce and imperious disposition.

As their mouths wrestled and their hands frisked fitfully, the heat travelled unbearably through her body. She could hardly stand a minute longer. The lust inside her yearned for more and a timeless bubble engulfed their bodies. But this time it wasn't just a purely physical joy enthralling her nervous system, it was more, much more and beyond words. This time it was the soul itself searching union.

Clinging to each other they held their breath in unison as if to stem the tidal onslaught of time and prolong their dream. Only this wasn't a dream any more. These were two real bodies yearning for each other. Having gifted past untold realms of complete pleasure to one another, Julia was ready to shed her clothes and his, and take their passionate encounter to a full circle.

"Make love to me, I love you", she heard herself mutter as he gently lowered her on the couch, his mouth still pressing on hers. The fragile intimacy of the moment took them both by surprise. They lay motionless entwined in a timeless embrace, languidly savouring every second and allowing the unbridled pleasure to go on forever.

"You mesmerise me. You're so beautiful. You do things to me", he groaned. He delicately uncovered her gracefully firm breasts, contemplated them broodingly and caressed them with the palm of his hand. Then he cupped them, pursed his lips and like a baby avidly sucked at her nipples. She groaned in pure pleasure and felt a huge lump in her throat.

"Yes." she croaked. "Oh. Franco. How I missed you."

"I know." His pulse jumped and his taut fingers squeezed on her femininity, then released them gently pinching her hard nipples as if working dough. She groaned again this time more vigorously. The flames burning inside her grew with each second. Her thighs trembled expectantly. She raised her heavy lashes and her dazed eyes were met by the astronomical hunger of a raging bull.

"I do love you, Julia", he said unsteadily. "I need you".

Passion ran through her, sensations of every form and colour blazed in every muscle, spreading exquisite agony, enslaving her to the master lover spawning this crushing cataclysm.

"Take me, Franco." It was an impulsive entreaty willing the floods of ecstatic joy to continue, to flow even more brutal and take her to the special place she so desperately wanted to be.

"I want you. I need you." she groaned repeatedly.

"Yes, yes."

The expensive scent on his parched body had now diminished and her senses were enveloped by an overpowering replacement of male primeval sweat. His skin glistened, his stiffened muscles hardened even more as she drove her fingernails into his back leaving a trail of long crimson lines.

He seemed to know exactly what she needed, where and when. She kept willing him on and on. She wanted to be satisfied like never before to make up for those long, miserable weeks she had reluctantly spent longing for his touch, those dreary mornings when her dreams evaporated into nothing. They had been unbearable weeks when all she could think of was bitterness and despair. Even when she had stood in the middle of her shoe shop, staring at her new inanimate companions, it had all been make-believe, all pretence, a feeble attempt to lift her languishing soul. Since her idyllic week in Milan her heart had never really been invested in her venture. Back in England her life had been insufferable and woeful. How she had survived the brutal ordeal, she would never know.

Franco's head gradually climbed till his mouth found hers again and his eyes met her pure emerald gaze.

"Don't close your eyes." he huskily said.

"I want to look into them, into your soul."

She stood still surveying the enthralling power in his dark gaze as a cold shiver ran down her spine. Then his wet lips pampered the nape of her neck causing reckless shards of indescribable frenzy to her system. She pressed him even closer to her and entwined her legs around him.

"I love you", she muttered. "I really do".

Suddenly, he pulled himself away, took a deep breath.

"You are something else, you know." He stood up, walked to the drinks cabinet and poured them another Cognac.

She shook her head still spellbound in a sea of primeval magic, enraptured in a whirlwind of hugely satisfying passion. She contemplated his beautiful body which only seconds earlier had made hers feel his equal. She had just experienced an uplifting trance that banished every negative thought. So she was more than a little confused when he stopped and withdrew so abruptly.

She took the drink and sipped it gently. "Thanks." she whispered hazily. An acrid taste trickled down her throat and a touch of disappointment appeared in her eyes. She had so desperately hoped they'd go all the way and make love all day and all night. After such a masterful curtain-raiser it seemed the natural thing to do. The foreplay was pure bliss. He had driven her crazy as she anxiously longed for the full force of his masculinity. But why had he stopped so cruelly and pulled away? Could his state of mind have anything to do with it? Though he looked perfectly fine to her.

"Thank you, Julia, for being here. You just don't know how much it means to me."

Her blood had run a little cold now. Her disappointment was palpable yet she wasn't regretting anything or thinking of digging more into his perplexing action. She was grateful he cleared some of the unanswered questions which had been plaguing her. Now she was as sure as she could be that she did love him, and he loved her. His eyes didn't lie. Neither did his body. It was no ordinary body to her or to any woman. Here was a man the likes of whom many women had dreamt of but never met. He had walked into her life, not only her love life but her professional life too. She had fallen in love with him and very likely the same fate had befallen him too.

"Thank you." she said wistfully, lifting her brows. She needed to keep her feet solidly on the ground and not jump the gun. It had been a truly, exceptional evening which had revealed a lot to her about him and herself too. They had both taken a further step in their difficult relationship, becoming a little bit more intimate with each other. They were bonding nicely and their friendship was growing too. She couldn't believe the long way they had come since that awkward introduction in her shop.

"I better call you a taxi. It's getting late." he said politely, his eyes lost on her as she brushed her hair to get ready.

Chapter 9

The next day the sun wondrously stretched its golden fingers to the horizon. Julia thought she'd wait for Lindsey before opening any more boxes. She had promised her to take some time off and come and give a hand in the shop but as yet there was no sign of her. Julia was also expecting the delivery of some large mirrors to compliment the elegant furniture she had already acquired.

She glanced at her watch, paused, and then directed her thumb to her lips, gliding it gently and thoughtfully over her mouth, but she soon snapped out of the of temporary daze. She decided to work on her inventory, categorising every pair by type, size, colour and price followed by gracefully positioning each left shoe on the empty shelves. After a while something seemed to distract her again, it had indelibly hung to her mind and wouldn't leave her. She sat down and picked up a magazine. But she couldn't help not dwelling on the events of the previous day. Hard as she tried her heart swelled every time her eyes lifted from the glossy pages and travelled from shoe to shoe till they finally shut to mull over the unmistakeable figure of the extraordinary man who had turned her life upside down.

Soon Lindsey and the mirrors arrived simultaneously. It was important they chose the perfect position for them where they would be most effective in creating the impression of unfettered space, a cosy well-being and graceful luminosity. The three ingredients Julia believed would persuade potential customers take the risk and walk into her shoe wonder world. That serious matter sorted, they closed the shop and walked across the square for a quick coffee.

"He wants me to go away with him for a weekend", she said.

"Go where? Italy? Paris?" Lindsey sounded so excited you would have thought it was she herself who had been the lucky recipient of the invitation.

"Well, we're not sure yet." She ran her fingers through her hair and ordered a large Cappuccino. Lindsey wanted a Latte.

"We're not sure yet?" Lindsey's eyes popped out of their sockets.

"Is this the royal 'we' already?" A few heads around them turned.

"Keep your voice down, Lindsey. This isn't a Press Conference."

"Sorry. So, you haven't been telling me everything then?" She looked and sounded cross. "You promised, damn it. I hadn't realised things had moved on so fast?"

"Slowly Lindsey, things haven't moved that fast at all."

"And who was that pretty girl with him the other night? Did he tell you? Was it an ex-girlfriend? Tell me, Julia."

"Lindsey, calm down. You're jumping to conclusions. Franco's brother Giuseppe died in Italy in a car accident. You've seen him at the restaurant. He was just a little older than Franco. That's why he didn't call. And that woman you saw the other night was Giuseppe's widow. So he wasn't seeing another girlfriend at all."

"Oh my God, how unlucky can you be? Is he alright then?"

"I think so. Franco is a strong man. But he's obviously devastated at the loss of his brother. They were very close, you know. Giuseppe died the same morning I returned from Milan."

"Oh how weird Julia. Isn't that a bad omen?" Lindsey's eyebrows lifted as if she tried to remember something important she had read somewhere. "Do you know his star sign?"

"Oh. Lindsey, leave it. Don't start with your silly superstitious theories."

"They're not silly at all, Julia. Star signs can determine the success of your relationship. And you of all people should know that."

Desperate to change the subject she dipped her face into her Cappuccino.

"I just wanted your opinion about something."

Lindsey's eyes stood still. She bit her lower lip and was all ears. "So, what's the question then?"

"Well, shall I go?"

"Go where?"

"Lindsey, haven't you been listening? He's asked me to spend a weekend with him."

"Oh, that."

"Well?"

"Well, I don't know. It depends."

"Depends on what?" Julia was sounding a little annoyed and impatient. "I went over to his palatial mansion yesterday here in Bournemouth."

"You didn't, did you?" Lindsey's shock once again drew a few bemused glances.

"No, it's not what you think. Just for a drink. He appeared at the shop unexpectedly and drove me to his. Okay, we kissed and cuddled a little. But that was it."

"So, you don't know where he wants to take you then?" Lindsey squinted at her pensively, pulled out her nail file from her bag and started rasping her nails.

"Does it matter where we're going or what star sign he is, for heaven's sake?" Realising her tone of voice was now out of control, she looked out for any heads turning her way. Then she glanced at her watch and went on rather feebly. "Should I go or should I just decline?"

"What do you want to do?"

"Well that's why I'm asking you, silly." She shook her head in disbelief.

"But you're going with him, not me, Julia." She dropped her file into her bag, pulled out her lipstick and applied a soft coat.

"I suppose I do want to go. He's been through a lot lately and I think he needs company." She pondered her coffee briefly, and then raised her eyes to an ominous dark cloud hanging over them like a sort of giant parasol.

"He needs your company?"

"Yes, he told me so, Lindsey." She hesitated resting her eyes once again on her coffee. "I like being with him. He has this magical effect on me. He lifts my spirit and when I'm with him I feel I can accomplish anything. Nothing seems too big or too difficult." Her voice dropped and a peaceful lucidity filled her eyes.

"Then I'd go with him to the ends of the earth. Even to hell and back if he's so amazing. You'd be a fool not to."

The elderly couple sitting at the next table turned and exchanged a polite smile. The man said something unintelligible which his partner quickly frowned at.

"He mentioned the lakes or maybe somewhere in Scotland", said Julia.

"I'd have thought Paris or Rome would have been more romantic. Don't you think?"

"I suppose so. But Scotland can be idyllic too."

Lindsey looked at her watch and got up to her feet.

"I need to run a few errands, Julia, while I'm here. And I promised my mother I'd go to M&S to look for this particular skirt she wants. She can't seem to find it anywhere else. Wish me well. I'll pop in later for a pair of posh Italian boots perhaps." They both chuckled, paid the bill and Julia returned to her labour of love.

The shop opened its doors to the public on the Saturday without too much fanfare. Franco was there and Lindsey and Lindsey's mum, a cast of celebrities performing at the Bournemouth Pavilion and Southampton Playhouse, local newspapers, a bevy of photographers, owners of boutiques, restaurants and cafés from the vicinity and of course a top DJ from Radio Solent. The Mayor did the honours of popping Champagne bottles, confetti and a barrage of flashguns and that was that. It was Julia's happiest moment and she wanted to cry as she sold her first pair of 'stivaletti' to the mayor's young spouse.

The following Friday Franco and Julia spent most of the afternoon driving up north on the M6. It was a long way to Fort William but the countryside was spectacular. The rolling green plains punctuated with clusters of grazing sheep and the solitary smoky cottages speckled at regular intervals. A wash of red sunset lingered beyond the sleepy hills on the horizon. Feelings of the romantic kind tickled Julia's nerve ends. The sense of expectancy inside her grew with every minute when Franco turned to her as the car came to a stop and kissed her, first on the cheek then on her lips, he aroused a huge tightness and an army of little arrows zipping through her stomach.

"Shall we make love in the car?" he joked. "It'll be different in here. A little uncomfortable, granted, but wow. It'll be memorable. Don't you think?"

She flinched in total shock. She had never made love in the back of a car or in the back of anything for that matter and she had never as much as contemplated the idea, not even in her wildest youthful exuberance. But she didn't think he meant the back seat. The way he said it, it seemed more likely he wanted the action on the front seat in full view of any curious passer-by.

"What?" She asked feebly. She felt humiliated by the vulgarity of the invitation. What if someone stopped to peer at them? What then? Would they just stop in mid act, pretend it was normal behaviour and wave graciously?

"Julia. Living on the edge is much more exciting than doing every single thing by the book. As you get a little older it is those wild moments when you let your hair down, stretched the rules a little and took calculated risks that you'll remember fondly. Not the rest of your humdrum life."

"So you'd call this a calculated risk?"

But before she had finished her question, he insulted her even more by running his hand over her breasts pressing them brutally, setting off stabs of pain rasping through her.

"You'll love it Julia. It's more exciting than doing it in bed." He laughed but neither his words nor the laughter could relax her stiffened body. She took an incisive breath and helplessly held her midriff. The heat inside her exploded like scorching lava flowing deliriously through her veins. He pulled her bra down and sucked her nipple while his hand rubbed her thigh.

"Franco." she cried out in joyous pain. "Please. I don't like this." she lied. But her face said otherwise as he was quick to notice and he savagely taunted her frail aching body a little longer. It gave him untold pleasure touching her curves, running his hand on her smooth untainted skin and seeing her aroused and ecstatic.

"Oh, I know you're enjoying every second of this." he said through his teeth. He replaced his hand on her heaving breasts, viciously sucked her neck and bit into it till she cried out. As he pulled his euphoric face away he noticed he'd left a crimson love bite mark on her neck.

"Oh, I didn't mean to do that, Sorry."

She stared at him vacantly. "What did you do that for?"

"I couldn't help it, Julia. You just drive me crazy every time I look at you", he retorted.

"Go on, let your hair down. Life is there to be lived to the full and that's what we're going to do this weekend."

She was close to tears but refused to give him any more satisfaction so she fought back. How could he humiliate her in such an inane manner in full view of passers-by? But thankfully there were none. At that moment she felt like driving off on her own and going back home. But she was so crushed and weak she wasn't even sure she had the strength to carry her small suitcase to the cottage he had rented for the weekend.

Carry her suitcase she did as she promptly followed in his footsteps, up the steep hill, into the narrow pathway and across a gravely front yard. The view was nothing short of idyllic and magical. A vast sea of incandescent colours washed the disappearing horizon. It could have been a Monet or a Matisse, she thought. She had to hand it to him. Franco was in a master class of his own when it came to exquisite and expensive gems, be it scenery, his suits, jewellery, wines, diners, anything under the sun really. She couldn't think of anything he wasn't cultured in. His words of advice were gold nuggets. Everything he touched turned to gold. He must have had the perfect breeding in Italy and the education normally only accessible to princes. How else could he have turned out so neatly sophisticated, accomplished and so complete?

As they dumped the suitcases on the bed she thought of slumping on the large four-poster herself. She was shattered.

"Well, there's time for a quick shower. Then we're off to a jewel of a restaurant I've hand-picked myself for you." The statement came laced with a regal smile. "It's just outside Glencoe."

Shock jolted Julia to the core. She could not believe her ears. The words in her mouth froze. They had only just arrived after what she thought was an exhausting journey. Surely he was tired too. He'd done all the driving himself.

"Not unless you want to make love before we go?" he taunted with a bewildering look in his eyes.

"No, thank you." she said unevenly. "Don't you ever get tired?"

"No, of course not. I do sleep at night when I can", he said with a harried grin. "That's the way God meant it. That's why there's night and day. But I do cheat sometimes, and have a little siesta."

"Well it's almost night time." She swallowed. Look the sun has almost set."

"That is true." He replied judiciously. "But it isn't night time yet. Anyway, six to seven hours are more than sufficient rest for a healthy body."

"Six hours?" She reeled. The little ordeal she had been subjected to in the car was already forgotten. She got her evening dress out and ironed it meticulously. She ironed his white shirt too even though it was brand new, straight out of the box.

The evening at the restaurant was enchanting so was the artistic décor and the food. It was a truly perfect evening and she couldn't have asked for anything better. It was an enthralling, romantic night. It gave her the rare opportunity to peel away the accretions of his posh education and his proud, condescending exterior and bask in the cosy warmth of a noble soul. He was a man of real worth and the more she got to know him, the more convincing she found him and the more spellbound she became.

Back in the cottage that night, they sat cosily by the fire only intermittently breaking the silence. They sipped a twenty-year-old Scottish Malt Whiskey and dreamily stared at each other.

"Oh I think I could get used to this", she purred. "But I don't think I could stand the winter here. I'm more of a beach and sun person."

"That makes two of us then." His voice was husky.

Before they knew it the night was into the small hours and Julia could hardly keep her eyes open. Her eyelids were heavy and her head was so nebulous she could hardly think straight.

"I think I'm going to retire, Franco. My head just can't take any more. Thank you for a magical evening. It was perfect."

He smiled at her and nodded. She stood up, kissed him and staggered into the bedroom, half expecting him to follow her.

"Good night." he said as his fervent eyes glinted indulgently at her curvy frame. He smiled blissfully but had no intention of making love to her that night. He could see she needed the rest. So he sat down again and picked up a magazine. It was another hour before he finally went to bed.

The following morning he cooked a full English breakfast. She sat down, sipped her coffee, propped up her chin on her clinched fists and watched him, motionless.

"Are you okay?" His quizzing eyes smiled at her.

"Yes, I'm fine."

She was tempted to ask him why he hadn't made love to her the previous night. It would have intrigued her no end to find out what his reasons were. It would have been the perfect follow up, in her book anyway, to such an exquisite and romantic evening. Even though she was tired, it hadn't stopped him before. The evening would have been even more memorable. There is always room for a perfect dessert even after a big meal. It's that proverbial icing.

"Did you sleep well?"

"Yes, thank you. And you?" There was a trace of caution in her voice. Julia was completely unaware he hadn't slept in bed. He had spent the entire night sitting on the couch, enjoying the quiet solitude in the knowledge she was safely sleeping next door. He did manage to nod off a couple of hours and that seemed sufficient for him. No one would have noticed any different. He looked fresh and bustling with energy but for a negligible hint of red in his left eye.

"I did manage to steal a couple of hours but then I don't need much sleep. It's one of those things. As long as I get those fifteen minutes in the afternoon, I'm fine". He spoke in that impersonal tone of a seasoned solicitor excusing the idiosyncratic behaviour of his client.

"Can I ask you a question?" Their eyes met for a second but she couldn't hold his powerful gaze for much longer. She sipped some more coffee and got stuck into her bacon and fried eggs.

"Yes, of course, and what about?" He glared at her expectantly.

"You know when your brother died, I know it must have been a devastating shock to the system and terribly distressing. But why couldn't you share the terrible news with me? It would only have taken a few seconds."

She instantly drew a painful breath and her eyes froze as she noticed the anguish in his eyes grow. She realised she had just opened a wound that was obviously healing slowly. Or maybe hadn't healed at all. Numbness swiftly spread to her limbs and face. She instantly regretted she had mentioned it and watched with a mixture of fear and apprehension as he looked around the room.

She certainly knew how to choose the right moment.

"I know I should have but the truth of the matter is I didn't." he said with a matter-of-fact flatness. "But that doesn't mean I didn't think of you every hour and every minute of the day. The image of you was always present and in a way was a source of strength for the emotional void left by Giuseppe. We were very close, you know. We were never apart and always worked together like a team. The bond forged between us was inseparable. I guess." He smiled sadly. "We were good together and made a success of everything we put our hands to. The day he died, after I had made the funeral arrangements, signed endless documents, I sat by the pool thinking of you. And that is the plain truth."

With tears flowing down her cheek she let out;

"All I needed was one little call. It would have made all the difference".

That afternoon Franco took her for the once in a lifetime experience. He hired a motorboat and two fishing rods. She had her first fishing lesson. At first she dreaded it, especially when the afternoon tide came in and the bumpy waves slapped their boat mercilessly. She had always been scared of little boats. But the moment she saw the little snapper juggling at the end of her line, she went delirious.

"Franco." she screamed. "Look. Look I caught one."

"Well done," he patted her on her back and kissed her on her cheek. Then he expertly released the snapper and hurled it back into the water. Her joy wilted watching the prize of her fishing prowess vanish into the deep.

"I know we could have made some nice fish soup", he said reading the disappointment on her face. "But I think it deserves a second chance, don't you?"

"Oh." The rocking boat was starting to give her sea legs. But they soon moored the boat and returned to *terra firma*. Her head kept thudding pitilessly and she thought she was going to throw up.

"I'm not feeling well, Franco. I think the waves have upset my tummy and I feel terrible nausea."

"Poor girl." he teased. "And there I was thinking you'd make a great sailor."

"I'm serious, Franco." It was a drooping tone which had lost its earlier vigour. "I think I'm going to throw up."

"We better take you to the cottage then", he said bluntly.

"It's little boats. They always make me sick. Not the big ones though. I'm alright on the ferries."

"Why didn't you tell me then?" His voice hit her like a whip. "You could have taken some seasick tablets. Here, you better put this on." he said as he threw his pullover over her shoulders. "It'll keep you warm."

He drove fast up the hill and into the country while she sat uneasily next to him. His driving wasn't helping in any way and was making her feel worse. But she didn't want to say anything. She prayed she could make it back to the cottage without having to stop the car to throw up. She inhaled deeply and stopped breathing hoping it would stabilise the funny sensations ravaging her stomach. Moments like these made her hate him. He seemed so patronizing, insensitive and a million miles away from her even though he was there, sitting next to her.

In a way she hated herself even more because the fishing trip was meant to be a real treat, something totally different from what she was used to. Maybe he had planned it to test her nerves, a ploy to build up her self-belief and a useful weapon to combat those awkward periods of insecurity. She had failed. What was he going to think of her?

When they got back to the cottage he pulled her close to him, kissed her on her forehead and smiled lethargically.

"You better go to bed", he said implacably. Then he dropped a small red packet into palm of her hand. "Take a couple of these pills and you should feel better."

"I'm sorry, Franco. I guess I'm not a good sailor." The pain weighing down the words said more than the words themselves.

"Don't worry about it. At least we caught something." There was a softer nuance to his tone now and somewhere buried deep in his hard glare was a little morsel of sympathy.

She hurried into her bedroom, swallowed a couple of tablets and sunk straight into the large bed. She just didn't know what to feel and with a stomach like hers, there was not much she could feel except dreadful nausea. She slept like a log the rest of the evening and through the night. When she eventually opened her eyes it was morning. Franco was in the kitchen preparing a continental breakfast, looking as fresh and chirpy as ever.

"Top of the morning." he said. "How are you this morning?"

"I feel better, thank you," Her head still heavy and fuzzy.

"Good. You look good too. Nothing too grand this morning, I'm afraid. No bacon or sausages, just a couple of croissants, some orange juice and a cup of coffee. How does that sound?"

"That'll be nice."

He seemed to have completely forgotten the unsuccessful fishing trip. It was as if it hadn't happened at all. A new day with a huge orange globe on the horizon was already smiling outside their window.

"If you're up for it, we can take a walk in the country. The fresh air will do you good."

She nodded. The stiff rigidity of her face relaxed and her green eyes smiled cosily at him.

"Good." she said. "Yes I think I'm ready for a good walk." She wasn't going to allow anything spoil the day this time. Not a headache or even an upset tummy. She wanted to make it up to him and show him what she was really made of. Moreover she wanted to prove to herself she still had the strength and perseverance that had helped lift Lindsey out of her purgatory. How else could she have come all this way?

As they walked up the hill the view of the vast blue sea below was exhilarating. The cold salty breeze caressing her nostrils fortified her body. It was precisely what the doctor ordered and there was a reassuring spring to her step. This was a healthy lifestyle she could adopt more regularly.

"So, how's 'Just Grace' doing then? You haven't mentioned it at all. Good I hope?"

The words hit her like bullets, cold and calculated.

"Oh, fine. It's doing fine."

She didn't really want to talk about it. She had been infinitely grateful for his sterling assistance in launching her into the challenging venture but now she wanted to do it on her own. She knew she was competent and could take care of herself. Anyway she would soon persuade

Lindsey to invest more of her time. Failing that she could always employ someone. But she didn't really want him involved or else it would soon become his baby and she would be left walking in his shadow. There were moments at the grand opening the previous Saturday when she felt his shadow eclipse her completely. She was genuinely thrilled he was there but wished he'd acknowledge her dream as solely hers. 'Just Grace' was her idea and hers alone and that's the way it was going to be.

"Just fine, that's it?" A ferocious frown contoured his face and his eyes popped out like lighthouses dispatching alarm signals. His tone of voice was uncompromising.

"How are the shoes selling? Have you had any write-ups in your local papers? You must have had some glamorous celebrities come into your shop."

She drew a long, deep breath wondering what had hit her. She tried to walk a little faster, avert her eyes pretending she was admiring the view, just to avoid his demanding eyes. But their close proximity made it impossible.

"So? Tell me about it. I want to know." he enjoined.

"Well, yes. Business is thriving. I've had a few important customers, a couple of comedians' wives, that blond girl who does the weather report on telly and a Kate Winslett look-alike but no Julia Roberts and no one from Hollywood yet. So, things have been good. I'm very happy."

"Good, I'm pleased for you", he said, his tone still brusque. "But you mustn't sit on your laurels, Julia. That'll be a huge mistake. I know I may be sounding a little condescending. You're only a novice, after all, in the world of business. The moment you become complacent or careless, that's when things start going wrong."

"Franco, I'm not a little girl. I think I know what I'm doing and where I'm going. You learn as you go along, there's no substitute for experience. I'm not saying I'm not grateful for your help but I do have a knack of doing things my way and I do have a vision too."

"I wasn't trying to undermine your achievement?" His double-barrelled shot sliced through her with lethal venom. Her head thudded and her ears quaked. He held out his hand and stiffly grasped her by the arm. She could not avoid his glare beaming at her.

"It was just a brief word of warning, that's all. So many businesses fold soon after opening because they can't sustain the initial success. They make the big mistake of thinking success will continue to flow automatically. But it doesn't. Only constant hard work, high standards and forward planning does. You can't afford to sit still."

"Franco all I'm saying is it's time I stood on my own two feet, that's all. I want to give myself a real chance to develop my own ideas." Her voice was hard.

"No one is taking that away from you."

"I know, but …"

"Julia, in business, team work and partnerships are essential. If it wasn't for my brother Giuseppe working hand in hand with me, I don't think I would be where I am today. And that's the simple truth. I didn't know this then. But I do now."

She stared at him for a long second fearing the mention of his brother's name would summon up pangs of grief and distress once more. Sure, he had provided the crucial contacts but it was she who had managed the transactions and bargaining. It was she who had set up the shop, discovered the perfect site and created the décor and the name. It was she who had to convince her bank manager her dream was feasible and worth something.

"It's not that I don't admire your grit and your tenacity", he went on, holding her chin in his hand so she couldn't avert his gaze this time. "That is very creditable. Why else do you think I like you? Apart from your good looks, of course, and the sexy legs and those toffee lips", he teased. "But the truth of the matter is, in the cut-throat world of business you need friends especially those in high places. On your own you'll fold like a deck chair, collapse on your face and incur losses you couldn't even repay."

"So you want to be my partner then?" she asked.

"No, no. That's not what I said at all, Julia." He frowned. "All I told you was not to isolate yourself. Don't go filling your head with a misplaced delusory sense of achievement. Full stop. No more, no less. End of story."

Without even a hiatus, his mouth alighted on hers and left the piercing imprint of a lingering wet kiss. She was so taken unawares by his sudden gesture she froze on the spot, cold and delirious at the same time, lost somewhere between the bliss of the Garden of Eden and bedlam of Babylon, yet where exactly, she could not tell. All she knew was her legs beneath her gave way, her heart stopped and then thumped unevenly and a sea of arousal cramped every muscle that stitched her body together. She was fond of little surprises but this one surpassed them all.

The evening they skipped dinner and made sweet love instead to the sound of Michael Buble'. It banished her headache and every other ache that beset her enfeebled body. She even shed a few tears during the night lying next to him without knowing exactly why.

"We'll have to do this more often", he said huskily before he nodded off. "What do you think?"

"Yes, I think I'd love that", she said caressing the back of his head.

"Maybe we could go to the island of Skye or the Isle of Man", she demurely suggested. But her words fell on deaf ears. He seemed so docile and vulnerable lying asleep next to her.

"I love you", she whispered and kissed him on his mouth. Then she rested her head on his chest--this lifted with every breath he took like a gentle wave. She felt so powerful next to him, so buoyant, brimming with confidence, with vigour and hope. Every breath he took aroused sweet sensations inside her and set off dreamy expectations of a fantasy future shared together. "I surely do, sweetheart."

He took a larger breath lifting her head on a higher wave. She stiffened for a long second thinking he'd heard her and was about to respond in similar fashion. But it was a false alarm. She smiled at him tenderly and showered his uneven chest with myriads minuscule kisses.

She wondered what sort of amorous images his sleeping mind was unfurling. She too let her imagination take her on a fanciful journey to a still world, where love was sugar-sweet and starry-eyed forever. But love and friendship were difficult bedfellows, she thought. Love and friendship could so easily get in each other's way and when they did which would the victor be? It was a dangerous partnership but one which nonetheless offered amazing rewards, did it not?

"I hope you love me too", she muttered. She sighed deeply and on that ambivalent note slept peacefully like a baby.

Setting back home not a second after six, the next day had them back by midday. He dropped her at her house, gave her a wave and drove off.

Hardly had she left the shower than the phone rang. It was the familiar voice of a livid and excitable Lindsey.

"Why did you switch your mobile off?" she complained with some bitterness. "I've been trying to call you all weekend. For heaven's sake, what if something happened to you, Julia? I was worrying like crazy? I even watched the news thinking maybe you had an accident on the motorway."

"Lindsey, I'm fine. What's wrong with you?" It was painful listening to her motherly screeching. "For God's sake we only went up to Scotland and you knew that anyway." It anguished her to have to justify her every movement. "Lindsey we wanted a quiet weekend away from all the hustle and bustle. That's all. So we both switched our mobiles off. It's not like you didn't know where we were."

"Yes but ……. It would have been nice to know how you were getting on." The harshness in Lindsey's voice turned soft.

"We really got on fine. He took me fishing." she laughed.

"Took you fishing, what, with a rod and line?"

"Yes in a boat. We hired a boat in Fort William. I even caught a little snapper." There was a spark in her eyes. "But we threw it in the lake again. It was small. Apparently that's what they do."

"So, are you feeling better now?"

"Yes, thank you." Lindsey's tone was bleak.

Later that morning they had their usual coffee, talked some more about Julia's weekend and Lindsey shared a little gossip from the travel agents. The evening, after tea while Julia was watching the news Lindsey rang again. She sounded all agitated and breathless.

"What is it Lindsey? Are you alright?" asked Julia all calm and collected unable to work out what exactly could have happened in a few hours to have distressed her so much.

"Julia, I saw him again."

"What do you mean? Saw who?" she croaked, getting confused.

"Franco, I saw Franco. I saw him with another woman at a bar today. They were having a drink at a bar near the Odeon cinema. It wasn't the widow. She was younger."

"Oh, why are you doing this to me, Lindsey?

"Because ……. because I care for you," Her voice emotionally loaded.

"Lindsey, Franco runs a popular restaurant. He must meet loads of girls and just because he has a drink with one of them in public doesn't mean he's having an affair with her, does it?"

"Well no. But we don't know that, do we?"

"Lindsey, you are unbelievable. Give the man a chance for heaven's sake. I told you it's me he loves. I know it now." Yet the flat tone of her voice failed to convince Lindsey.

As she hung up she wondered whether her friendship with Lindsey was coming between her and Franco.

Chapter 10

Lindsey's latest disclosure tormented her all day. Either way she would soon find out but until then she really didn't want her much needed hours of sleep to be hijacked once again by unproven suspicions. Who could it be if it wasn't Giuseppe's widow? It had to be a new waitress or a barmaid perhaps? But why would he meet her in a bar? The restaurant would have been the correct venue for a professional interview and Franco was known for his professionalism. She felt guilty of this arousal of distrust towards him. After all he had done for her, the latest weekend in Scotland still fresh on her mind, and was it not high time she started to trust him, unreservedly?

She didn't sleep a wink all night and was wondering how best to broach the matter. Could she just ask him point blank? That approach had already proved embarrassing once. Better still she should ignore the whole thing, and move on. She certainly had enough on her mind with the long hours in the shop, keeping the books in order and getting new orders in for the successful 'stivaletti'.

A few days later she picked up the phone on at least nine occasions, but each time her reasoning told her otherwise. It seemed Franco's extraordinary patience and cool-headedness was rubbing on her too. Finally she did call but only to thank him for a splendid weekend and to apologise for her unfortunate sickness.

"We'll have to do it again soon", he said. "You'd like that, wouldn't you?"

"Yes, of course", she chirped. "Maybe next time we could go to an island somewhere."

"An island sounds good to me. Do you have any suggestions?"

"The Isle of Man maybe or one of the Scottish Isles?" she added rather flatly, maybe hoping he might mention his mystery girl encounter.

"An island it will be then, perhaps somewhere a little warmer and more exotic."

For the next two weeks there were no calls from either of them. Both were completely wrapped up by their punishing schedules to have the time for one another. But there wasn't a day that Julia didn't think of him or the mystery girl, and this was continually eating her up. She knew her suspicions would not go away, despite her growing trust in him, not unless she nipped them in the bud.

Having closed the shop she called Lindsey and suggested a night out in Poole, starting at Franco's restaurant, enabling them to carry out a little clandestine investigation. Lindsay was prepared for anything.

As they walked into the restaurant there was no sign of Franco or the girl, only the regular staff.

"Is Franco not here this evening?" asks Julia trying to sound as nonchalant as she could.

"No, not tonight." answered the good-looking waiter who fancied Lindsey.

Julia seemed quite surprised.

"Why?" beamed the waiter. "Was he meant to meet you here?"

"Oh, no, we're just passing by. That's all."

"He always comes over to say hello." Lindsey could not take her eyes off the waiter.

"He must be busy tonight."

"Have you taken on new staff at the restaurant? Is there a new girl?" Lindsey's idea of diplomacy was a little different from the norm. For her, going straight to the heart of the matter seemed to obtain the swiftest results, sparing everyone unnecessary anxiety. In this instance even Julia, in spite of her initial apprehension could see sense in such an unorthodox strategy.

"Not that I'm aware of," the waiter frowned, turning his head as if looking for someone then shaking it.

"In fact I'm sure we haven't. Mr. Rocco always informs the staff whenever there are changes or new people coming in. I would be very surprised." He scratched his head and chewed. "Why do you ask?"

"Erm...." stuttered Julia.

Lindsey's eye-lashes flickered and she smiled suitably.

The waiter's eyebrows lifted and a bright spark left his eyeballs. Then, as if following a brief thought process he nodded.

"Was the woman in question in her thirties, very pretty, long jet-black hair and large blue eyes?" He lifted his finger off his chin and smiled somewhat smugly, "and a nice tan?"

"Yes, sounds like her. Do you know her then?" Lindsey's voice revealed her euphoric surprise.

"Well no, I can't say I know her but I do know who she is. I've met her."

The two women waited with bated breath but the waiter got suddenly distracted by a beautiful red-head, genteelly escorted into the restaurant by a tall man with shining dark brown hair and very well attired.

"Will you please excuse me, ladies?" He swiftly floated across as if on roller skates and showed the couple to their table, beautifully laden with red roses. He then popped a bottle of the finest Champagne and deftly poured it into their glasses.

"You see, Julia, I told you. You always think I make these things up, don't you?"

"Lindsey, I never said I didn't believe you." Julia said bleakly. "I only said you're too sceptical and quick to judge Franco. You don't know him."

"And you do, do you?" Lindsey snorted.

The waiter returned holding a menu. "Sorry about that, ladies. They're regular patrons and very fussy too." He handed over the menu, explaining as he did so the specials of the day.

"So, can I get you an aperitif?"

"I'll have a Campari and soda please." said Julia.

"You didn't tell us who the mystery lady is?" Lindsey, and Julia to a lesser degree, was dying to find out the true identity of the mysterious girl and the nature of Franco's relationship with her. She had to unravel this mystery and quickly for Julia's sake. She wasn't going to allow Franco dupe her dear friend into a sham of a relationship and set her up in his harem of beauties at the mercy of his fanciful whims. Then dump her at will at the advent of younger new models.

He hesitated as a smile best described as cynical elongated his mouth.

"Why are you so interested in this woman, may I ask?"

"We're just curious, that's all." Lindsey's resilience refused to cower.

"My friend thinks Franco is having an affair." Julia sniggered point blank, giving Lindsey some of her own medicine but equally eager to get to the bottom of the tedious matter.

" I see," the waiter yielded to a hearty grin. "No, no, nothing of the sort. Franco is not that kind of man. He's always been a family man and since Giuseppe's death if anything he's become much more hands on with his relatives in Italy.

The lady you saw is Giuseppe's widow's sister. Her name is Claudia and she's come over to be with her sister at this difficult time". His face was now sober and his voice heavy as his telling eyes set on Lindsey. "

You'd think the waiter had been paid to produce such an eloquent character appraisal for Franco. This was indeed praise fitting for a saint and not a successful businessman in the restaurant trade. But fitting praise it was and Julia could not contain the extraordinary joy overwhelming her heart as she listened. Her eyes desperately held back the tears. Thankfully the waiter had left with their order.

"I'm happy for you, Julia. I'm really happy." She hugged her for a long moment and added almost pleadingly. "You know I really care for you. I just wanted to make sure you didn't get hurt."

"I know." Julia choked. "I guess, better safe than sorry."

The following day an unexpected customer stepped into her shop. He stood at the entrance just looking around, marvelling at the stylish collection of footwear almost like a child in a sweet shop.

"Hello Julia. I was going to call but what I had to say to you is much too special to be said over the phone." Franco stood still smiling at her without the slightest overspill of excitement. It was a considered smile, one which carried good things. But the mysterious joy in his eyes was more obvious and Julia's heart started to beat more briskly. She had loved surprises from a tender age but surprises from Franco were in a totally different league.

"Franco, you always choose your moments well."

They were the only words she could think of in the circumstances. Every second felt like an hour as she stood motionless. Her throat was dry and her face shocking pink, matching the boot sitting unsteadily on the palm of her hand.

"Keep next weekend free. I've a little treat for us. I've found an island which I'm sure will thrill you to bits. And no, it's not the Isle of Man and it's not off the Scottish coast. It's somewhere a little warmer, more rustic and more remote. An island inhabited by no less than the gods themselves."

"An island inhabited by gods, where could that possibly be?" A deep joy powered her limbs and she instinctively ran up to him and threw her arms around his neck. "I don't think I can wait."

"Neither can I Julia. But as they say, good things come to those who wait or something to that effect."

He helped her lock up and they went for a drink across the square. The pub was busy and loud but they found a little quiet corner where they could actually converse without the need to lip-read.

"So, are you going to tell me where this idyllic island of the gods is?"

"It's meant to be a surprise, Julia. But I've given you a little clue. Do your homework." His tone was that of a school teacher teasing a listless student.

"It's not Crete, is it?" Julia had studied Mediterranean geography at school and she did recall a handful of islands closely linked with ancient Greek mythology. Crete was certainly one."

"You can try but you will not guess this one. If I were you I'd wait." He serenely folded his arms and grinned. "By the way, the girl I had coffee with in town the other day is Giuseppe's sister-in-law. She's here for a month to help out. That's all."

"Yes, I know. Lindsey doesn't miss a thing, I'm afraid". She was about to tell him in spite of everything, she did trust him and in her heart of hearts she never really doubted him.

"Julia, tell me. When are you going to start trusting me a little?" His eyes beamed a ray of charm giving her skin goose bumps. She swiftly lowered her gaze but words failed her. What could she say? She didn't want to lie to him.

"Soon", she whispered, her heart slumping under the weight of her guilt. "I promise". She feared that if she didn't prove it to him soon and beyond doubt she might lose him. She knew he liked her a lot but his patience wasn't infinite.

Also admittedly there were many other fish in the sea. After all he was a hugely attractive and powerful man. Loads of girls here and in Italy would give their right arm to have him. She had to stop allowing Lindsey running matters of her heart. Only she knew what she felt and what she really wanted. She also knew perfectly well that without trust no relationship could survive for very long.

"You promise do you?" he teased.

"Absolutely yes, I do Franco." She took a deep breath. "But I don't want to lose Lindsey. She's a long standing friend and one of the rare breed."

"I'm sure she is. A friend like her should be treasured and treated with the greatest affection."

"She's finally accepted to help me at the shop. So I'm really grateful to her." Then, in a more relaxed tone she added. "And we're also going to employ another girl."

"Good." Franco nodded, "a very wise move."

The following Friday they flew to the George Cross Island of Malta in the heart of the sun-kissed Mediterranean. Julia was over the moon as she gleefully surveyed from her window seat the vast sheet of blue beneath then the fetching blue-eyed man by her side. Before she had time to take in the full span of this dream holiday, they landed in Malta and were swiftly whisked off to a waiting helicopter. Within ten minutes they were settling in their hotel room on the idyllic island of the gods. It was none other than the island of Gozo, a rock with more history and mythological connections than most islands anywhere in the world. Gozo was more than a dream come true. It was the elusive dream she had never had. Having had no expectations she felt like Eve in the Garden of Eden, living with the gods. Everything on Gozo was steeped in history and much rolled back into the dark annals of myth and prehistorical. There were the churches looking more like Cathedrals with exquisite murals and frescoes by the likes of Caravaggio. Then what Julia found most thrilling was a host of underground and open-air temples inhabited by giant stone gods and goddesses which had survived the scourge of a Great medieval Siege and two World Wars. At a place called the *Ggantija* stood an impressive headless goddess who hadn't been so fortunate.

The limestone houses had doors of different colours, shapes and sizes and never seemed to close, day or night. The oversize bronze doorknobs too were a graceful work of art. The friendliness pervading the villages gave the impression they were inhabited by one great big happy family. In fact in-laws, grandparents and all manner of relatives lived within a couple of doors of one another.

But what really captured Julia's heart were the elderly ladies, devotedly nestled on their front door steps from dawn till sunset, knitting flowing woolly pullovers or making intricate lace tablecloths for discerning tourists. She fell in love with them the moment she set foot on the amazing isle. She even sat next to one of the gentle elder ladies, hands clasped over her knees, listening to the hardships they had endured on the island during the Second World War. The lines and dark shadows that ran furrows across her face were a living testament of a past and of severe suffering.

What Julia found even more interesting was the uncanny fact that though the people of Gozo seemed to jump out of the pages of an ancient history book, they all seemed to understand and speak good English. The contrast could not have been more extraordinary.

That night Franco booked a table at one of the top restaurants on the historic isle. It overlooked a popular beach the locals called *Marsalforn* and it was equally popular for there wasn't one free table in the house. The atmosphere was friendly but also loud and festive. But they knew they were in for a treat when two serenading minstrels approached their table brandishing guitars, a generous glass of red wine and a smile that would have charmed any princess. They played some local folk songs, asking for special requests as they hopped from table to table, regaling the guests.

Julia leaned forward and perching her arm gently on the table, kissed Franco.

"Great choice." she said with glowing eyes.

"I guess it is." he said, running his fingers through her hair. "But it's not quite what I had hoped for."

"Why?"

"I thought it was going to be a little more intimate and romantic."

"Oh, but I love it, Franco. This is an island you'll never forget. I can tell."

"And you haven't seen anything yet, Julia," He hinted with eyes of someone who knew more than he was prepared to admit. Not a flicker, just a cool distant gawk surveying her reaction.

"Well, that's partly true but you know the little I've seen so far has been such a wonderful education, I think I could stay here forever."

"Well, you mustn't rush into anything now. There are still thousands of beautiful islands you haven't seen yet."

His chest lifted as if to gloat of yet another mysterious surprise he had up his sleeve.

"But are there enough weekends in the year to visit them all?" she queried, wondering what his impish mind was cooking for her.

"Probably not, but then that's why one has to be discerning and choose the rarest bijou. The way I chose you", he added without a flicker of emotion in his voice.

"A bijou," she pricked her ears quite bemused by the unfamiliar sound of the word.

"Yes that's French for a jewel."

Astonishment locked the word in her throat. But she looked at him in suspense, it was at that moment when the waiter pulled up at their table with the order and the minstrels approached once again with a medley of local folk serenades.

"Do you do Beatles' songs?" asked Julia hesitantly.

They gladly obliged with a rugged rendering of 'She loves you." and "All you need is love." As they listened they tucked into their main dish. Franco had a local fish, the Mediterranean answer to the river trout announced on the menu as a *"Lampuka"* while Julia indulged in her delicious fillet steak.

"Before I forget we need to get you a sunhat tomorrow because you're going to need it."

"Where are you taking me tomorrow then?"

"Time and place for everything", he retorted coolly. "And I guess this is as good a time as there'll ever be for what I've to say next. Maybe not the best place but I'll say it anyway."

Julia suddenly held her breath.

"I've been waiting to tell you this for a while now but didn't quite find the right moment. I don't just fancy you, Julia. I do love you. I love you a lot. I know this might be hard for you to believe, but from the very first moment I set my eyes on you I knew you were the one. Yes and my guess is you love me too or else you wouldn't be here with me, would you?"

"I guess not," she croaked. But she couldn't quite say the magic words.

"Darling, I always knew sooner or later you would come around. And Milan was that moment, granted with a little helping hand from mother fate."

His disarming eyes gleamed and the warm touch of his fingers on her hand sent blood surging through her veins. She never imagined being in love would be so completely overwhelming. It not only sent sweet sensations through her every muscle in her body but every inch of her brain was elated by a sudden stream of shock waves she couldn't even start to describe. It was the purest form of joy which sealed her bond with Franco like no other. Her sandy green eyes were alight.

"But then in every walk of life everyone needs a little helping hand from somewhere. Ours came from above."

Franco stood up; his chest lifted with pride and stretched his hand out to her, gently pulled her out for a dance to the accompanying strains of the moustached minstrels. Her pulse was racing and her body quivered. She surveyed a sea of eyes fixed on her like spotlights. Spiralling waves of heat enveloped her as she floated in a wonderful daze. In spite of her initial reticence a pure joy filled her heart. It was a delicate touch that caught the eye of most of the patrons who applauded the impromptu virtuoso performance.

"I'm a proud man dancing with the most beautiful girl on the island," he whispered into her ear, taking a playful nibble as he spoke.

She held him closely as her weightless body followed his lead. She wasn't quite sure what was happening to her but whatever it was she wished it would go on forever. If ever she had entertained any doubts about her love for Franco they had been instantly dispelled. Only he could make her feel the way she did. The heights of passion and excitement his firm touch aroused in her was uncontrollable.

When they sat down again Julia felt like a celebrity. Once the limelight left their table, they looked into each other's eyes like two lovesick adolescents who had kissed for the first time. For a brief moment she considered how lucky she had been to have met him and how badly she had misjudged him on their first encounter. If it hadn't been for those celebrity shoes of hers they would probably have never met and their love would have never seen the light of day.

"So what did you think of me the first time you saw me? Why was it me and not Lindsey or one of the many beautiful girls gracing your restaurant?" She finally found the courage to ask.

"Something told me you were the one, the moment I set eyes on you. Your legs did stand out, have to admit, so slim and elegant," he teased.

This wasn't quite what she was expecting.

"But what really did it for me was your face, your voice and, of course, your warm smile. A girl who smiles is ten times more desirable to a man."

He kissed his fingertip and placed it on her lips.

"I know diamonds are a woman's best friend and all that. Yet to me a genuine smile from the heart is more precious than a diamond necklace."

"But for a woman smiles and diamonds are inseparable", she said mockingly.

"What I'd really like to know, Julia," he added, looking at her intently, "is when you actually fell in love with me." His tone was now crisper, feral even.

"That's easy," she said. "It happened in Milan when I watched you dive into the lake to save that young boy. It was such a brave and selfless thing to do and you didn't even hesitate. Until then I wasn't sure if I even liked you. But it was probably the most daring thing I've ever seen anyone do." Her eyes misted up as she spoke. "It was something you expect to see on television. But this one was happening in front of my very eyes. I felt so proud of you. You instantly became my hero."

"Hero." he jangled. "I'm your hero. That is the best thing I've ever heard. I think I'd like to hear that again, if you don't mind."

She gladly obliged, this time with more pizzazz. She glanced at the revelry around them and for a fleeting moment it seemed as if she and Franco were the last two romantics stranded on this idyllic island where the mythical Calypso allegedly found love. As if it was fate herself that had once again contrived the magic of their special evening, a beautiful young girl with flowing chestnut curls who couldn't have been older than ten blithely hopped into the restaurant carrying a basket of roses and strolled up to Franco. She stood in front of him and held up a red rose while a perfect set of white teeth smiled at him.

"A rose for your beautiful wife, sir?" she finally asked.

Franco gave the young girl a generous tip, took the rose from her hand and offered it to Julia. She was so touched she was really struggling fighting the tears now. Gazing into her eyes he ran his fingers tenderly on her silken lips. "You know Julia, you're such a natural beauty you took my breath away the first time I laid my eyes on you. And every time I look into your eyes it feels like it's the first time again."

The honest passion in his piercing gaze always had the same effect on her and this time it was no different. It sent scintillating sensations flooding through her body. Within a few moments as they left the restaurant she floated weightlessly in his firm embrace. She was speechless but the joy in her eyes spoke volumes.

"Thank you for an amazing evening," she said.

"It was the best evening of my life."

"I had the time of my life too, you know. But don't speak too soon", he gurgled deep in his throat. "Tomorrow is another day and the way things are going, who knows what's in store."

The following morning after breakfast, she slipped on her swim-suit and a light, cotton dress over it. At reception she found a large straw hat waiting for her. It had been delivered earlier by the paper boy.

"Have a nice day." wished her the receptionist.

They hopped into a waiting taxi which drove them down a steep hill, flanked by vast golden cornfields. Then the taxi climbed up again through a narrow lane which opened up into a large dusty square with a huge Church dominating the cluster of limestone houses around it. Once again the veteran ladies were in evidence assiduously knitting away on their door steps. What a sterling example they were, thought Julia, for the up and coming youngsters on the island. But where were the young people of Gozo, she wondered? She hadn't seen many children playing in the streets or in the shops. The flower girl was the only person under twenty she had seen so far.

But things soon changed when the taxi pulled up next to a jetty at Marsalforn Bay and stopped. A burly bearded man in a white vest waved at them from his boat. It didn't take Julia long to work out where the day would take them. Thankfully there were no fishing rods in sight. But the equipment in the boat looked even more daunting to her. Her stomach churned.

"Have you ever been scuba diving before?" yelled Tony the boatman as the engine roared away and the boat left the jetty.

"No never." Julia was determined not to let her delicate stomach get the better of her this time. She was going to enjoy every minute of this exciting experience. As a young girl at school she had always been fond of watching deep sea programmes on television. But diving with the fish was something she had never envisaged doing herself. This was indeed overwhelming.

Franco had been to a few diving expeditions in Egypt but it had been a few years since his last dive. So he too was looking forward to the trip. A few hundred yards to the west of the jetty Tony dropped the anchor.

"Since you're a novice", he said to Julia, "we'll have to start in relatively shallow waters. We'll see how we get on."

He explained to both the underwater sign language and started helping his two guests with the rubber suits. Then he expertly slipped their oxygen tanks over their heads and secured them tightly. When they were both safely rigged up he put on his own equipment and all three somersaulted into the water.

As Julia had her first brush with a life fish she was so thrilled she almost forgot to breathe and started to panic. But Tony swiftly calmed her down and held her hand till she seemed in charge of her own movement. Then all three together explored the rocky sea-bed. Clouds of little fish darted past them with no particular destination and an array of different coloured fish gathered around them gaping at the human visitors to their world. Some of them held no fear. Others, especially the silvery ones just vanished into the distance. A few striped ones drifted unperturbed.

It was like swimming in an aquarium but better. There were slippery snappers, squids and an array of multi-coloured fish scurrying below them and large crabs crawling on the sea-bed. She dived to touch the spiky sea-urchins. At that moment Tony pulled out a penknife and showed her how to yank it off the rocks. He then cut it open and showed her the edible orange bits.

As they slowly explored deeper waters a couple of chipper dolphins appeared from nowhere and frolicked around them like roguish kids. Julia just could not believe her luck. One of the dolphins nudged her and she had enough time to caress her slippery coat. Meanwhile Tony kept a close eye on proceedings just in case the dolphin got too friendly. Franco watched closely behind. He wanted Julia to be the protagonist for the day. This was her day as far as he was concerned.

Their time was almost up. Tony indicated there were five minutes left before they would resurface. This was the cue for Franco's next move. As Tony retreated Franco hovered in front of Julia, calling her attention with his hands. She shook her head unable to comprehend what he wanted. But without wasting another second of their expiring oxygen, he pulled out a little red box, opened it, picked up the glittering ring and gently secured it on her finger. Julia thought she was going to faint.

When they were back in the boat and no longer inhibited by the heavy equipment, Franco kissed her lovingly.

"So, will you marry me, Miss Julia?"

She nodded unable to utter a single word.

"Yes," she eventually said with tears of joy flowing down her cheeks.

"I've waited a long time for this," he enthusiastically replied, "but it was all worth the long wait."

"This is the happiest day of my life," she muttered, "I promise I'll be the perfect wife."

His arms tightened around her, "and I the perfect husband." His voice was unequivocal. He then released her, picked up her straw hat, hurled it far into the water and asked Tony to take them back on terra firma.

That night there were no dinners in fancy restaurants. They had a quiet supper at the hotel, ordered a bottle of Champagne and two flutes and went back to their room. Franco wanted the night to be theirs and theirs alone without any moustached intruders serenading his treasured possession. What he wanted to do that night was for her eyes only. They made tender love over and over again. There was an endless stream of unspent passion waiting to nourish their unfathomable love.

"My mother told me, you know....that one day I too would be happy," She cried, running her fingers through his thick hair. "I never believed her. But I do now."

"Well, that makes three happy souls then Julia, my love. She's probably watching us right now."

They closed their dreamy eyes and kissed with a ravenous appetite which grew with every passing second. The night soon bowed its head to the light of day as a stunning orange globe climbed in the stainless blue horizon. Julia sneaked out of bed and tottered up to the window admiringly.

"It's the most beautiful sunrise I've ever seen." Her glowing face bewitched by the solar disk crossing the horizon and its accompanying atmospheric effect.

"It's like a painting every artist would want to paint."

"That may be so", Franco strutted up to her and tenderly squeezed her body close to his.

"Unfortunately I'm not an artist. Though looking at you in the warm sunlight, I do see one. But what I'd like you to create for me is not a painting of a beautiful sunrise. I'd like you to have our beautiful baby."

Julia's eyes filled up and her throat seared as he held her in his arms and showered her with tender kisses. She wished time could stop and the immense joy of that blissful moment would last forever. She had so often dreamt of moments like this but none could ever match it. This was truly magical and a baby would be the best way to prove their love.

"If it's a boy we'll call him Frank Junior." There was a whole lot of love in her crackly voice.

"And if it's a girl", he enthused huskily, "We shall call her Julietta."

The End

Printed in Poland
by Amazon Fulfillment
Poland Sp. z o.o., Wrocław